Praise for *Double Crossed*

"If you're writing a 'novel of ideas,' you'd better not neglect the novel for the sake of the ideas. You have to do all the work you'd put into a novel of entertainment. You have to develop real characters. You have to have imagination and much narrative skill, because if the book does not make the reader feel the action is taking place in the real world, the ideas you're trying to convey aren't going to impact the real world the reader actually lives in. It has to be "novel" first, "ideas" second, for the ideas to make their maximum impact. Lucky for us, Brian Sloan managed to figure this out all by himself! You're going to be forced to think, and you're going to enjoy it!"

—Robert McNair Price, author, *Deconstructing Jesus*

Double-Crossed:

The Imperium Impugned

By Brian Sloan

Harvard Square Editions
New York
2015

Double Crossed: The Imperium Impugned, copyright © 2015 by Brian

Sloan

Cover Photo by Vito Fusco ©
Cover design by Michele King ©
Editors: Geoff Smith & Laura Driver

Published in the United States by
Harvard Square Editions
ISBN: 978-1-941861-05-9
www.HarvardSquareEditions.org
Printed in the United States of America

Prologue: Falling Stars
Abu Hamed, Sudan

This night they saw one falling star.

Abdikarim and his older sister, Zeneb, were snuggled atop the eggplant and ochre–dyed throw. The missing archeologist had abandoned this very blanket just a few weeks before this brilliant moonless night. The kids were gazing up at the stars on the outskirts of their small, desolate village beneath a gently sloping ridge next to the Nile.

"Look!" Abdikarim insisted, directing his sister's gaze. "There! You see it?"

"Yes, Karim, I see it."

"Dakka B say it a person moving to the heavens."

"I know, Karim, I know. You always tell me that."

Abdikarim shifted his focus from the heavens to the blanket. He grabbed it and tried to lift it to his nose. "Get off it! It's mine!"

"He gave it to both of us!"

"Off!" Abdikarim yanked with a resolute might.

"Stop it!" With a swift countermeasure Zeneb rose, yanked on the blanket, and pulled it right out from under him. Towering over him, she giggled.

"Therici!" he screamed.

"That's not even a real word."

"Is too! Therici!"

"Stupidici."

"MINE!" Abdikarim shrilled.

"Here, take it. You just want to smell it? That's weird, Bojab."

"I tell Mom you call me that."

"You don't know what Bojab means."

"Do too, Therici! Bojab."

Abdikarim took the blanket from Zeneb and brought it to his nose, relishing the lingering scent of his friend Dakka B, the archeologist.

It was the archeologist who had given him hope; it was the archeologist who taught Abdikarim simple lessons about the planets and stars, and Abdikarim missed him dearly.

After a few moments of smelling the blanket, Abdikarim placed it almost exactly where it had been and plopped onto it. "I share it with you now!" he said, patting the vacant spot next to him.

Zeneb sprawled beside her brother, and both returned their focus to the stars, searching the sky for more people moving to the heavens. Zeneb picked up a fold of the rough blanket to scratch the intense itching that fired in her every nerve. They'd both been itching for weeks now, since around the same time Dakka B departed and the small black fly transmitting the river blindness arrived.

"You scratch it raw. Mama say no scratch!"

Zeneb kept scratching. "What you call that star there? The one were Grandpa and Papa live."

Abdikarim started digging into his own forearm, near his elbow, with his cherished pencil. Here in Abu Hamed, a pencil was a rare and valuable possession.

"I not see grandpa's star now. Dakka B call it Nort."

"I love stars. But I miss the moon."

"Some time moon sleep."

"I wish I could."

"Mama say men fix us today. No more itch."

"She said it takes time. And she scratches too."

"Mama hit me."

"I know, Karim, I know. You're always in trouble."

Zeneb thought of the relief the end of her itching would bring and managed a genuine smile. Smiles here were scarce. Then she punched her brother hard—for no reason, just like any older sister her age might. He scowled and grimaced, but her defiant stare cowed him from retaliating. Like kids everywhere, their emotions were exaggerated. Their sourpuss expressions conveyed the unspoken threat that they'd never speak to one another again.

And then just seconds later, Abdikarim said aloud, but just to himself, "Wonder what Dakka B do?"

He imagined Dakka B holding the sun, keeping it away, cooling them so they might sleep. He imagined him returning triumphantly to save the village from the other villages that he'd witnessed invading before.

And then with the limited attention span of a kid, he returned to stargazing and scratching the lesions on his skin.

And then they were startled by annihilation's muzzled woof. The stars disappeared, obscured by a thick layer of vaporized dust.

They both bolted up, choking on particulates. Their shocked looks spoke their thoughts. They crested the hill that had blocked the view of their village, only to see that everything was gone. The dust that swirled in the air caked their faces and bodies was what had been their village, their family, and friends. Everything, everyone, turned to dust in an instant.

Impressive! Gotta love the latest in nanoenergetics, thought the man who had claimed to be an aid worker with the WHO. *And with just a backpack and a button, no training. That backpack made the whole damn place just disappear, just like they promised it would!*

As the man and his fellow "relief workers" stood watch just beyond the now-obscured Nile, he spotted something move in the haze just on the other side of where the village had been.

"Pasqua, come with me! Antonino, keep your position."

The two aid workers rushed to their motorized raft, hopped aboard, and sped to the opposite bank. They clambered out of the raft and raced across the desert sand, unholstering their Glocks without missing a step.

A Glock would more than do when the enemy was armed

with only a pencil.

"Where did our home go? What happened?" Zeneb was the first to speak once the aid workers were near.

Karim rushed to the man who called himself Pasqua. Crying, he latched onto his leg. In his mind, he was grasping Dakka B's leg.

Am I being rude by not answering her question? the button pusher wondered. *It sure sounded like a question.* He trained his gun on the little girl's head, walked up to point-blank range, and pulled the trigger. Her head exploded.

"My turn!" Pasqua laughed. "Hey kid, get the hell off me! Maybe you got some stupid comment to make like she did, the one with the hole in her head … What, you don't understand me, you stupid savage!"

With a violent kick of his leg, he bucked Karim loose.

Then as the little boy lay there sprawled on the desert sand, his terrified, dusty face streaked with tears, Pasqua kicked him in the throat.

Despite being utterly terrified and sobbing, Karim mustered one last heroic thought: *Maybe everyone move to North Star …*

"Hey kid, this should cure your leprosy or whatever that is!"

Pasqua laughed again as he pulled the trigger. In fact both men were laughing as Abdikarim's brains splattered near his sister's onto the desert floor.

Just a few days later, the leader of the death squad had returned to his home and was showering, attempting to scrub his most recent mission's thoughts from his memory, when his phone rang.

Twinkle, twinkle little star, how I wonder what you are. Up above the world so high, like a diamond in the sky …

It was his boss's ringtone. He knew it well. Although this was the first time the ring had ever made it to "diamond." Usually he'd answer before the second "twinkle."

"*Pronto!*"

"Queen's Park Rangers," his boss advised.

His boss's last tip had been a bad one, but he never considered giving the man hell. Instead he did what he always did: said "*Sí*" and immediately disconnected the call. Perhaps it was that his boss had hit the previous 47 tips in a row. Or maybe he just knew better?

In the beginning when his boss called with just the name of a soccer club, he hadn't bet at all, but was wise to note the outcome. After the first four tips hit, he bet conservatively, just €1,000. Last week he had given a little back, €100,000. His instinct demanded that he pass on this latest tip, but QPR wasn't playing until tomorrow so he had some time to decide.

With his hair still damp, he flopped onto his sofa, flipped the TV on, and settled in to watch his beloved Lazio take on the team he detested most, the side from Torino—Juventus.

I hope he breaks his leg, he thought.

He was thinking of Ta'Nessi Assad, the young star striker on Juventus. Assad's last-second goal the week before had cost him that €100,000, ending his winning streak at an implausible 43 bets in a row.

Early in the second half of the match, just as the button pusher finished his leftover pasta, Assad collapsed onto the pitch. No one was even near him; he just collapsed on his own accord.

The camera focused on the fallen star. Thankfully he rose. He managed two or three steps before collapsing again. The camera zoomed closer. Assad's face was contorted with a look of pain and panic.

He again made it to his feet but collapsed before his first step. He grasped at his life as he struggled on the turf. His body convulsed with violent spasms as he held tight to life— for perhaps too long, to the horror of the viewers watching.

Finally, he lost his grasp. The Tunisian, whose fitness and health were constantly monitored, had died of a heart attack.

Okay, maybe I will bet €50,000 on QPR.

Chapter 1: Hear the Piece

Oh Fortune, like the moon you are changeable, ever waxing and waning; hateful life first oppresses then soothes as fancy takes it; power and poverty, it melts them like ice.

Fate—monstrous and empty, you whirling wheel, you are malevolent, well-being is vain and always fades to nothing, shadowed and veiled, you plagued me too. Now through the game I bring my bare back to your villainy.

Fate is against me in health and virtue, driven on and weighted down, always enslaved. So at this hour without delay pluck the vibrating strings; since fate strikes down the strong man; everyone weep with me!

—*"O Fortuna,"* author unknown, early 13th century

The luminous white moon—marred by massive gray zit scars—was a motionless wheel. Its rays shimmered on undulating waves below, casting a dazzling brilliance against the otherwise dark, tempestuous Tyrrhenian Sea.

Ciro Pane watched the lights of the slumbering cities on the Amalfi coastline. Gerardo Purpo was all but asleep at the prow.

On this particular evening roughly three miles from their picturesque home port of Praiano, these two best friends were praying that a tuna might find their fishing lines. They had faith, but not in a mystical wheel spinning in the larger cosmos. They trusted in God, and the circumstances of their time and place labeled this trust Catholic. Soon enough, they would realize that this faith was an imaginary impediment, for their conductor had already cued the orchestra and the choir: *O Fortuna … Velut Luna … Statu Variablilis!*

Gerardo sought a larger yellowfin tuna by setting his lines at a depth of fifty meters. When his descending line was nearing the target depth, he sometimes yodeled *O di ludi O di ludi O di ludi Oohh*. The yodel was always the same and reserved solely for when he really needed it.

This night, he yodeled … you couldn't top-troll the sea here; you must plumb the depths. Despite their normally voracious appetites, mature yellowfins in this area were more invested in migrating deep beneath the surface than in their feeding.

Gerardo had baited for the cherished fish with a writhing, fleshy squid that squirmed and glistened in the moon's rays, securing it on a bent dinner fork–sized No. 9 multi-barbed hook.

He had caught a 300-pound yellowfin the year before, near this very spot, though at that point he baited with skipjack and fished at a different depth. That was what he'd told his fellow fishermen, anyway. Curtailing competition through deception was simply a way of life in these waters.

Their boat, *IXQUS*, measured sixteen feet in length and was considered large for a fisherman's boat in this region. They had purchased this tangible seal of their partnership with the proceeds of a single bluefin tuna that Gerardo had caught years ago. Unfortunately the bluefin, which is far more prized than the yellow, no longer swam these waters.

IXQUS satisfied what they needed, but she didn't embody all that they longed for. Their dream boat was piloted via a pipe bar ending with a turn throttle that attached to a pull-start motor. But to most of the local fisherman, Gerardo and Ciro's motor was luxurious. The others rowed far out to sea, a mile or so, alone in tiny wooden boats with their lanterns lit to alert the passing cargo vessels that could accidentally ram them.

"Do you remember when we used to come out here for fun?" Gerardo asked. His speech, like everyone's from Amalfi, was a colloquial Italian that sounded like a dog barking. No Roman would have understood his Neapolitan-influenced dialect. "We didn't care what we caught, or if we caught anything at all. Now it's a constant struggle to stay alive. It's impossible to relax any more. I'm always rushing to find that next Euro—why did we convert to that useless Euro? It makes me sick just thinking about it. I've got nothing now, nothing …"

"You know you have more than most, Ote," Ciro replied. "A beautiful, loving wife and son. That's worth more than anything else." He held out the joint he was smoking. "Here, do you want to hit this?"

Gerardo, or "Ote" as he had been known ever since he returned after several years in *Thailandia*, frowned and sucked on the joint. Decades of fishing had taught him patience in the face of misfortune, but tonight the waiting was taking a heavier than usual toll.

"We'll catch something, we always do," said Ciro. "Maybe not tonight, but that's how it goes. No sense looking back— best to make do and accept what we can't control. Just look at this scar you gave me. You're always stumbling over everything—and usually hook-first. But I don't fret about your past blunders, or mine for that matter. I let the delightful Mary Wanna take away my woes!"

"No, I think I'm really going to get sick just thinking about it."

"Mary will cure that too! Just don't splash on me. In fact, let me back up a bit. Is it the rough sea that has your stomach turning?"

Gerardo leaned over his side of the boat with his hands holding firm to its rim. He wasn't really sick, but was prepared to act the part when he noticed *it* rising and falling in the sea like a bobbing boggart several hundred yards away. "What's that atop the sea over there?"

"Where?" Ciro asked.

"*There*. Between here and Germano." He pointed back in the direction of the moon, toward a familiar rocky celebrity that resembled a solider of Caesar's time. The object in the water was barely discernible, evident only from its faint reflection of the lunar rays.

"*La linea*!" Ciro shouted. "*Pallino!*" Gerardo's pole, static all night, suddenly bounced like a *pallino*—not a cue ball as the word meant in the rest of Italy, but in their southern dialect, an ultra-bouncy small rubber ball.

Gerardo made a joyous, graceful little spin and reached his pole before Ciro finished his *ea* in *linea*. With his sharp cheekbones and lean, muscular body, at that moment he resembled the Russian ballet dancer Rudolf Nureyev, who once owned the nearby islands. Gerardo's inexpensive reel squealed as it surrendered its line at a manic speed. "Tuna!" he cried out. "Monster tuna!"

Ciro moved swiftly to command their drifting boat, pulling the rope starter to his Mercury outboard. "Less drag!" he cried. "Your line's going to break!"

"Shut up and mind the boat! And get this other line out of the water before it's entangled."

With movements surprisingly deft for his age, Ciro advanced to the stern and quickly reeled in their second line. At the prow, Gerardo, a silhouette against the moon, let his line drag out. His voice was animated and now entirely unintelligible.

After what seemed like an eternity, Ciro glanced at his watch, noting that the fight was a mere five minutes old before the fish abandoned its line-snatching run. Gerardo had begun his characteristic dance, rhythmic steps reminiscent of the rumba, with the yellowfin as his dance partner.

His hips swaying with the sea, he lifted his rod, gradually augmenting the force of his heave then reeling frantically on the downward step. The bolero playing in a continuous loop in his mind was slow as he heaved and swayed and muttered *presto* during the reeling step. He focused on line tension and direction, intermittently barking orders to his captain.

"You're going to have to keep pace! Good God, what are

you doing? Keep pace, don't back off—follow it!"

"I am!" Ciro protested. "It keeps changing direction. Your drag's set too strong—back it off!"

"Do you ever listen? Can you not hear me? Do your job with the boat, please, and don't distract me—just hear me! Christ!"

The monofilament line heard Gerardo; he only had fifty meters absent with almost two hundred meters repossessed. Slow to crescendo, the leading male begged with erotic temptation while his dance partner teased.

By measuring the pressure on his rod, Gerardo appraised the fish. "It must weigh two hundred pounds!" he exulted. His pounding heart surged with yet another release of adrenalin. "God always answers my prayers. And just in time for a new fridge!"

The thought gave him the courage to ignore the intense pain in his arms and back. It had already been twenty minutes since he began tracing this relentless rumba with his feet.

The fish finally yielded to the human, floating to the top of the sea some ten meters away. It was theirs. But then it abruptly plunged deep beneath the leaden sea. Gerardo let the fish drag out the line once again—such fish can't be fought, but only worn out. The tedium of this second phase of sparring was beginning to show on his face.

When armed with a common rod like Gerardo's, conquering a two hundred pound tuna is comparable to a tourist hiking from what they call a beach here to Gerardo's apartment high on the cliffs above on a viciously hot August day. It's like climbing from the basement stairwell of the Empire State Building to the observation deck … when that tourist is a middle-aged smoker who sits behind his desk eating cupcakes by day and by night might thumb past a fitness show on his way from one of his favorite shows to the next. Gerardo wasn't a desk sitter, cupcake eater, or TV watcher, but he was a smoker, and his breathing now was labored and ragged.

But he was nearing the summit. He was once again overcoming the odds, nearing a victory that never failed to thrill him in precisely the way he most liked to be thrilled. But he was cautious not to stumble in these waning seconds. He remembered a time prior to his marriage when he had danced the dance of his life. He was patiently reeling in the stunning American tourist of college age. He had been only minutes from landing her too, but then he tugged too hard.

After another ten minutes, a somewhat less demanding encounter than the first round, the monster finally surfaced. The slightly choppy sea protected its secret an agonizing five or six seconds before Ciro demanded, "Is it a tuna?"

Gerardo answered with a rattle of expletives as if from an Uzi. He slammed his pole into the boat with a ricocheting clatter and collapsed, exhausted, onto the wooden bench seat. Veins were bulging all over his face.

Ciro patted his partner on the back, attempted a reassuring look, and hooked the monster grouper in the gills with a large grapple. He was angry too, jealous of the yellowfin tuna—worth nearly fifty times as much as this grouper—hidden beneath the water, their treasure that some other fisherman would claim.

"A great fight!" he said. "Brilliantly caught. Hey—it's better than nothing!"

Gerardo scoffed. "A damn grouper! A grouper, in June?"

They fastened the fish to the side of the boat, as it was too large to bring aboard. Gerardo's knot around the grouper's head indicated that he hadn't quite forgiven the hideous fish. His knots were tied with a hateful rage. Ciro was surprised, given the recent struggle, that Gerardo had the strength to hate.

Once the all but worthless fish was secured, Ciro carefully stepped over the two middle bench seats while constantly checking his balance with each step, choosing wisely to tightrope the non-grouper side, and grabbed a couple Peronis from his cooler. He splashed beside Gerardo, sporting that wide Ciro smile that caused his eyes to squint and brow to wrinkle. "Cheers, my friend! Well done."

"Shut the hell up, you idiot!"

Gerardo could say that and often did. Fifteen years ago, when they were thirty, they calculated that they had spent 5,478 days together on the beach. Ciro had done the math.

They began as five-year-old children playing in the rocks, aimlessly tossing them into the water. They would wade out and test the strength of the waves, hoping one would tumble them over. Then over the years they progressed to playing ball sports with their feet on the beach and working with their hands in the sea. Later, their marauding years honed their lean athletic builds, which they exhibited with endless energy.

Now they were men and, on an occasion or two when they were out and about, tourists would mistake them for enemies on the verge of a brawl, their hands flaring, voices loud and brisk, engaging in ostensibly heated exchanges. But what strangers often took for the prelude to a fight was merely their particular form of passionate debate, perhaps over a headline in the local paper or a controversial offsides call from the prior evening's televised soccer match. Such are the nuances of friendships nurtured over time.

Their once-enticing good looks were a few years behind them. They had long since abandoned the habit of arching their shoulders and sucking in their gut, often known as the Alexander technique, to give the illusion of a decidedly different profile. Advancing years and approaching middle age had taught them a refined, subdued assurance with their bodies—a physical assurance that, with time, had gradually cohered to match their mental poise.

So Ciro did shut up. They each knocked back three beers while listening to the silence and gazing at the stars. *IXQUS* was three miles off the shoreline when Gerardo, lying across the wooden bench in a near-fetal position with his head twisted awkwardly up, broke the silence in an uncharacteristically defeated tone.

"Let's go home."

Go home? Ciro usually put up a fight—he would reason with him, he would convince him. Like Gerardo, he had already imagined their pockets full of money. He even had imagined how he would spend it: he dreamed of buying a diamond engagement ring. But their dreams had been swallowed by the sea—at least for tonight.

After coaxing the motor to life with extra vigor, Ciro slammed the steering bar hard to his left and gunned the throttle, spinning the boat abruptly back toward the port. Then he noticed a large dark disk rising and falling with the waves. It was the same object that Gerardo had tried to point out just before their fight with grouper.

"What's that?" Ciro asked with a quizzical look on his face. The curiosity in his voice roused Gerardo from his pathetic fetal position on the bench.

"What's what?" Gerardo asked in a why'd-you-wake-me voice. He had forgotten that he was the first to see it.

"There! Over there! Is it a capsized Zodiac?" Ciro pointed toward the disk, which was now about thirty or so meters off their bow.

In spite of his less than enthused expression, Gerardo seemed to have shaken himself from the daze following his battle with the grouper. Gradually increasing his focus, he cuffed his hands around his eyes as if holding binoculars and scanned the dark water for the object his friend was so determined for him to find.

"It's just trash! There's always trash floating in the sea these days. No one cares about tossing crap into the sea any more, especially those damned tourists and their yachts. Correct your course and let's go home before I really do get sick."

Ciro just shook his head. The object, about three meters

in diameter, was a perfectly shaped disk. Trash was not this flawlessly shaped, nor would litter have inflated floats around its base. As he pulled the boat alongside it, he noticed a smaller disk perfectly centered on top. As he reached out to touch it, his first inclination was that they had discovered a UFO. It was matte grey in color and felt like it was made of PVC.

"What the hell is that?" Gerardo sputtered. "You might want to back off a little bit. Good God, what the hell is it?"

"Grab your pole!"

"You must be nuts! I used to think you were crazy—now I'm sure. Pull away!"

"Just get me the pole. Relax. It's not going to attack you. It's just a raft of some kind."

Even in the dark, the disk was obviously too large to retrieve from their boat. They attempted to secure it with a fishing pole, but the disk was too cumbersome to control.

"You must jump aboard the UFO—it's the only way!" Ciro insisted.

Gerardo cursed. "That damn grouper wore me out. I don't have the strength."

Ciro knew there was no value in arguing with his friend. Knowing Gerardo like he did, his battle with the grouper would give him an excuse not to do any real work for at least the next two weeks.

So it was Ciro who stepped off the boat onto the bobbing disk. It was as slippery as he imagined wet PVC would be. His foot shot out from behind him and hurtled toward the edge of the disk in a nosedive. He blocked his fall with his dominant elbow and bounced—more like a cue ball *pallino* than a bouncy *pallino*—off the disk and into the sea. The sting of the saltwater amplified the pain in his elbow and his left shin.

Gerardo huffed, doubled-over, doing his best not to laugh. Ciro cursed curt waves of invectives, softened only by the seawater's efforts to muffle him. His words first attacked the disk, then turned against Gerardo.

"You piece of crap! No-good slippery mother … I don't think this garbage knows who it's messing with!" He punched the side of the bobbing disk, stinging his hand, and glared at Gerardo. "What's so funny? You should be in here instead, but you waste all of your girly strength on a useless grouper. I'd have cut the line the instant that grouper started wasting my time. But you foolishly believe it's a tuna?"

But Gerardo was far too amused to take Ciro's insults seriously. From the safety and dryness of the boat, he mimicked his friend's failed attempt to board the disk. Finally Ciro flashed a smile and splashed seawater toward the boat. Then he returned his attention to the disk.

Humbled but determined, he spent the next five minutes calculating the best approach to boarding the disk, which had no handholds and was perfectly smooth. Each time he tried to pull himself up, it bobbed toward him and dumped him into the sea yet again.

Muttering blasphemies under his breath, Ciro heaved himself onto the disk yet again. He braced his feet against the side of their boat and scrabbled up. He let out a long satisfied sigh as his body and the strange craft bounced in unison with the sea.

Gerardo tossed him a rope, which Ciro slipped through the eyelet on top of the disk.

"Take that, you greasy bastard! And I'm talking to you, Purpo, not this worthless thing!" At this moment of triumph, the conductor's command of the orchestra and choir above was almost audible as he signaled them to unleash their stored energy on the climax of Orff's *O Fortuna* piece. Ciro hadn't just secured a disk; he had secured their fate.

"It's probably a bomb," Gerardo declared after helping to hoist his dripping friend from the sea. "One of those weapons of mass destruction!"

Gerardo was wary—many are on the Amalfi coast, when it came to the unknown. Many residents had met tourists who turned out to be their own special versions of weapons of mass destruction.

"We could be infected already, or at least I could be, but not by a bomb. UFOs must be radioactive too. But if there's tiny aliens aboard that I just rescued without any help from you, I'll be their hero and rule the world! Maybe this will persuade you to lend me your jacket so I won't freeze on our way home."

"You're not touching my jacket. It's brand new and not water resistant. Or blood resistant—look at your elbow! Your thin blood's everywhere!"

"What, this scratch? I hadn't even noticed. Jesus. Here, hand me that rag … I wonder what it really is. The bottom's deep, well under the water line."

"I tell you, it's a bomb. But whatever it is, it's dangerous to be sure. Did you see any identifying marks?"

"Are you kidding me? I couldn't see anything out there; I just heard your annoying laugh."

Ciro wrapped the rag around his elbow and they both intently scanned the disk, looking for any clue of its origin or purpose. "You know what I think?" said Gerardo. "I think it's a smuggler's disk filled with white owl!"

"Ha, we better cast it back out then," Ciro snorted.

Although they had learned essentially nothing more about the disk since they first spotted in the water, they still allowed themselves to speculate. Speculation, of course, never stayed within the bounds of the mundane. Their speculation was laced with gold.

They remembered well, from their early twenties, their own experimentation with the white owl that delivered euphoric insights, the absurdity of which was never acknowledged until much later. Memories of those exciting but foolish times brought them a renewed realization of the insidious power of the white powdery substance.

That only night the white owl paid them a visit was the

same night they ended up catching a couple of truly tantalizing trophies—two beautiful Belgian tourists. All had seemed to be going as planned for the two friends. That is until their wilted, lifeless, big-mouthed snakes starting talking to them. This one night of shame quickly shrunk any desire to indulge in the lure of the white owl ever again.

"Are you kidding?" Gerardo scoffed. "We wouldn't snort it—we'd sell it. I bet it's overflowing with white owl. That's got to be worth €10,000,000 at least!"

"Maybe it's filled with diamonds! Remember that South African yacht we saw earlier today? Naturally, a South African vessel's going to be smuggling diamonds."

"Either way, soon we'll be driving Ferraris."

"We'll live the life of Gio!" Ciro said, thinking of the richest person he knew.

"Let's open it up!" Gerardo exclaimed. Feverish with speculation, he showed none of his normal reserve or discretion.

"Out here? It's a slippery bastard … but you're right, of course. Where'd I put that screwdriver?"

"No, not here, you imbecile. Of course we'll take it back to Praia first. No one will be there, not at this hour."

On the trip in, they felt something short of total elation, for they still had no idea what they were dragging. For all they knew it was filled with canned grouper. After twenty minutes of fighting the waves, they returned to Marina di Praia, still entirely deserted as the clock neared three in the morning.

"Pull in over there by the dock, where it's shadowed." What Gerardo called a dock was really a rocky outcrop jutting into the sea.

"Are you going to be the crane that hoists this up? There's no chance, let's just bring it ashore."

"You'll have to get back in the water again—and no complaining, you're already wet."

"Are you sure you have the strength and know-how to

guide the boat over and tie it off, all by yourself?"

"Are you sure you are not as dumb as they come?" Ote scoffed. "Hop in the water and get to it! You're wasting time."

"You're right of course. I'll prove they don't make them dumber or more wasteful than me ... Look at me shivering—ah, this should warm me and maybe help stem the bleeding too!"

Before Gerardo could react, Ciro snatched his friend's barely worn jacket from its unprotected place on the seat near him and dove into the waist-high water some five meters from shore. Gerardo might have aroused the entire village with his full-bodied protestation of "No!"

And when Ciro surfaced, Ote continued in the same way. "Unlike you, I don't have a rich girlfriend. I have a wife and child that I must support. It's no wonder you're always smiling with that dumb smirk of yours."

Without bothering to reply, Ciro towed the disk to shore while Gerardo docked their boat nearby. Armed with a flashlight, Ote continued his resentful rant, and Ciro's smile only made him angrier. Together they struggled to drag the disk up the beach, though Gerardo was more focused on staying dry than helping. Not only was the disk's depth, measuring nearly two meters, considerable, it was also extremely hefty. About midway up the central body, a silver metal band flush with the surface encircled both the smaller and larger disks.

As Ciro attempted to gain leverage under the disk, he ripped the skin of his palm on a jagged, sheered cross at the disk's base. A closer look with the flashlight revealed four identical metal crosses, evenly spaced, fastened to the disk's foundation.

"Go get your tools while I stand guard and try to stop this bleeding."

"I doubt you have forgotten, Ciro, that you are the very proud record holder of the race up the mountain. Why, you can be back in a flash even if you sprint at half your record-setting pace!"

"My record will never be beaten, but why race up on foot?" Ciro countered. "You have the motorcycle record—take your bike! But neither of us will return in time—like always, you waste time debating instead of heeding my sound advice."

"Perhaps it's better if we just hide the disk for now!"

"Now you're thinking."

Ciro kicked the top of the disk, but it was sealed tightly and proved unresponsive to his kick. Gerardo, still worried about WMDs, especially now that the disk was completely exposed, jumped back in alarm.

"Go get the boat, you little girl!" Ciro implored. He liked to tease Gerardo; it wasn't the first time that he had called him a little girl.

Circling around the disk, Gerardo scurried across the black pebbles of the beach, never elevating either foot more than a few centimeters off the ground. Jumping onto the rock pathway, he walked rapidly to the boat. He gave a stealthy survey spin, a small attempt at reassuring himself that the coast was clear.

"Hey, get back over here, the damn thing's stuck, I can't dislodge it!" Ciro demanded. "Come on man, they'll be here soon!"

Gerardo ran back to assist Ciro. "So much for staying dry," he sighed, trying to time the calm waves to avoid getting too wet as he helped shove the disk back into the sea.

"Your arm must be broken!" Ote cried. "My wife likes it when I act like a little girl but I doubt Amalia does, seeing as how you're not even faking it!" said Gerardo.

"I've told you that I don't want to hear about the sick games you play with Juliana! Keep that hidden in your bedroom! Now where will we hide this UFO?"

They both considered what constituted the perfect hiding place. There were thousands of natural hiding spots along the rugged, craggy rock face of the cliffs that protected and housed the villages of the Amalfi coast. There were caves at sea level worth considering, caves that created pools of icy waters deeper within the cliffs. But each option was quickly rejected, for boats with tourists and locals scoured the coastline daily. Then Gerardo snapped his fingers. *"L'Africana!"*

The Africana was a club within a vast cave high on the side of a mountain. As the owner was his uncle, Gerardo had worked there for more than twenty years. Ciro agreed it was the perfectly secret spot, at least temporarily.

Gerardo hustled back to the boat where, seeing the grouper, he was again reminded of his earlier anger and personal defeat. Had it been a yellowfin, his heart would have danced and the disk would have gone unnoticed. In their haste, they forgot Gerardo's wet jacket, discarded by Ciro just a few moments earlier, now resting on the small black rocks of the beach.

They slipped around an outcrop of the shore just as Pasquale, a local octopus hunter, began the ride down the six-hundred-meter ramp that traveled steeply from the main coastal highway to Marina di Praia. For Ciro and Gerardo, it was one of those split-second escapes that left them both a bit breathless and strangely exhilarated. Panic-driven, Gerardo throttled *IXQUS* around the vertical rocky cliff towering some five hundred feet above them, obscuring the approaching fisherman's sight.

It was a short three-minute trip to the Africana in their small craft. Together they were able to drag the disk onto the rocky shelf that forms the perimeter of the Grotto Africana. Once on land, the weight of the disk was greater than they had expected. The same steel bolts that had opened Ciro's palm occasionally caught on the rugged surface of the grotto's rocky floor, but they ignored the pain and continued penetrating the darkness. Slowly and steadily they hauled their mysterious find deep into the chasm.

Ciro's flashlight illuminated an otherwise obsidian cave; the splashing sea and their deep gasps for air were the only sounds, and both echoed for several reverberations. Gerardo had the perfect spot in mind.

"Here! Behind this boulder!" Gerardo commanded. "But whatever you do, don't trigger the damn thing!"

This last task demanded the final reserves of their energy. With clenched teeth and faces tongue red, they pushed and pulled. Finally the disk, now stained with Ciro's blood, found its temporary home.

"At last!" Gerardo panted. "Let's go grab some tools and pry this thing open."

"Think for a moment. Great care and craftsmanship have evidently been dedicated to forming this container! Just running your hands over it convinces you that it's expensive!"

Gerardo attempted to interject, but Ciro silenced him with the raise of a hand and continued his line of reasoning.

"Let's come back tonight and take our time to figure it out. Better for us to be safe than sorry. In the meantime we'll return to Praia, sell the fish, and nothing more."

A crowd of about a dozen fishermen were at the marina when they returned. "Nice Tuna, Ote!" Pasquale hollered as they docked. The other fishermen gathered on the shore eagerly joined in Pasquale's laughter.

"I found this jacket—I'll sell it to you for twenty Euro, Ote!" goaded another. "It's a little bit ruined by the sea, but I'll trade it to you for that fish!"

Ciro couldn't help but pile on. "He was drunk before we even started fishing and fell from the quay! That's why we spent the last three hours battling this 'tuna!'" Everyone but Gerardo laughed.

Salvatore Pisacane, the statesman of the group and owner of much of Marina di Praia, including two of the restaurants, the hotel, the boating excursion company, and the fish market, moved purposely to the forefront of the rocky dock.

"What the hell happened to you, Ciro?"

Ciro stared back with a confounded look.

"You're bleeding! That fish must have put up one hell of a fight. The cost to repair your hand will exceed the value of the fish!"

This garnered a chorus of laughter from all those standing near. Those who hadn't caught Salvatore's jibe made sure to seek out those who did, yielding even more reverberations of laughter. Salvatore was correct that the fish was worth less than Ciro's hospital bill would have been, though Ciro would hold to his lifelong practice of letting time, rather than a doctor, mend his injuries.

"He was not even in the fight!" said Gerardo. "He fell on our way out—too much beer, always too much beer with this one! I always take the fish! So I asked him why he always gets half the money! His answer was throwing my jacket into the water! Maybe his girlfriend will buy me a new one?" This brought even more laughter from the fishermen.

They parted ways, Gerardo to his motorcycle, Ciro to his rusted, much dinged, two-door blue Peugeot, a fifteen-year-old contraption that was still quite reliable from point A to point B. Neither his blood nor the seawater could devalue the car's filthy interior, a space filled with spent packs of Dinah cigarettes, fishing lures, and scattered papers.

He reached into his shorts pocket for his phone and realized that he had forgotten to spare it from his adventurous dip in the sea. Better to go by Amalia's house anyway, he thought, returning his dripping phone to its soggy home in his pocket. He knew that she'd pacify his pain and mend his wounds.

Chapter 2: You Monstrous Wheel

Daybreak brought Praiano's charm into sharp focus. All the villages along the Amalfi coast were terraced into the mountainous hills that steeply plummeted into the Tyrrhenian Sea. Both vast and tiny villas, glamorous hotels, and all sizes of restaurants and shops dotted the vertical hillsides. Half of these structures were painted in vibrant shades of blue, yellow, purple, and red. These colorful buildings were balanced by stark white buildings. Every village was anchored by a gleaming Catholic church, either a *duomo* or a basilica, depending on the village.

In June, the mountainside was still green, dotted with grassy tufts of evergreens that clung precariously to rocky outcrops. Chestnut and oak trees reached further up the steep slopes, accentuated by clumps of wild rosemary bushes, and patches of heather with their signature flowers of pale lavender.

The sea was still, its brilliant blue throwing nearly blinding flashes of light back at the onlooking villages. The gentle ripples of the surface magnified the sun's intensity, achieving an effect of a million tiny flashbulbs intermittently igniting.

On this morning, Ote's wrath was also ignited. He had momentarily forgotten the disk, and awaking to the smell of rotting fish had put him in an equally rotten mood. His refrigerator had finally taken its last breath. No longer continuing with its normal purring, it now exhaled a decidedly rancid stench.

Once again he cursed the grouper. Last year's tuna was enough to sponsor his current ride, a 16-year-old Yamaha motorbike. Before that big payday, he had walked, took the bus, or caught rides with his wife in her car. Even with a car, parking was nearly impossible, so ultimately one walked the last legs of their destination. That's why Ote preferred the bus.

Buses dominated the coastal highway during the late spring to early fall, as the buses facilitated the tourist season. The blue SITA bus kept to the coastal road from Sorrento to Amalfi—it was too large to venture off its main path—and skirted the coastal cliffs where one mistake might make for a five hundred foot free-fall. Add the tour operators' buses and it was a veritable metaphor of coagulated blocked arteries. The traffic accentuated the hate facet of the classic love-hate relationship most locals maintained with the tourists.

Praiano claimed nearly three thousand inhabitants in its lofty nest. They all knew one another; indeed, most were related in some way. They valued their place on earth, their neighbors, their way of life, and most especially, the sea that provided for them.

What Ote hated this morning, in addition to Juliana leaving the rotting fish for him to dispose, was the reality that his motorcycle refused to start. He was taking the steps to work this morning and his muscles, still raw from his fight with the grouper, throbbed with each stiff step.

Around a blind bend nearly halfway to Marina di Praia, he was nearly knocked to the ground by a pair of tourists, zealous joggers racing up the stairway with their heads down. Rather than angering him, the incident sparked memories of his own legendary races with Ciro. Memories of his youthful days always brought a smile to his face.

Despite the late night, this morning Ciro was his usual bright, blue-eyed self. He strolled without a care in the world, except the occasional throb in his shin or elbow. Even those stabs of pain didn't detract from his affable mood, as they conveniently served to distract him from the constant, nagging pain surging from his bandaged hand.

Having arrived at work, he was slicing just-picked tomatoes under the large awning made from overlapping panels of tan canvas sails that shaded the small dining tables. Behind the bamboo wall that fronted the tables was the tiny kitchen, bar, and DJ control center, a space collectively known to many as the submarine. Those who worked behind the scenes rarely surfaced from their labor of making food and mixing drinks and music.

Ciro's mind wandered to thoughts of the mysterious disk tucked inside the cave—wandered so far, in fact, that he was lucky he didn't remove a fingertip as he sliced. In his typically confident way, he wondered what treasures the disk held and how they would transform his life when his attention was captured by Amalia.

By now she was hard at it, wiping down one of the orange sun loungers that formed eight tidy rows of seventeen. By day's end they would be scattered everywhere but for now all faced the sea. Immense boulders that had fallen from above made a haphazard seawall shielding the club and providing the necessary vertical face for the sea to effect its gentle splish-splash, further adding to the ambiance.

Matching orange umbrellas would soon be opened as the One Fire filled with tourists seeking an alternative to the blazing hot pebbles of the other nearby beaches. When walking down to La Gavitella from Basilica San Gennaro, the umbrellas emerged as gigantic bright orange mushrooms.

The path down to the beach passed several rocky outcrops from which the bravest could dive into the water, but the water's transparency daunted most tourists with thoughts of broken necks. The large boulders that rested on the seafloor more than thirty feet beneath the surface appeared much closer. Even those divers who had already made the plunge remained leery, second-guessing themselves because the illusion of proximity was so deceptive.

Ciro's illusions were far more graphic though equally misplaced. "Quick, Amalia—I need your help!"

She turned slightly toward him with a look of doubt, her

close-set almond brown eyes narrowing as she slowed her circular wiping motion. She opened her previously straight lips into a smile, revealing her quintessential radiance.

"I'm the boss!" Ciro reminded her in his signature demanding sarcasm. "Don't ever forget that!"

He was the boss when it came to One Fire, but in their relationship they were peers who moved as one. If anyone ever assumed the supervisory role it was Amalia, out of sheer necessity for the sake of Ciro's safety. He could be somewhat reckless, often spurred by challenge and competition, and goaded by Ote. Their current fascination was swimming out to a rocky cliff, climbing as high as they dared, and diving back into the sea just as they had done as teenagers. It was almost more important now, at this age, to outdo the other.

Amalia loved Ciro's playful nature, but most of the anxiety she coped with in her life was caused by his attempts to relive his youth with Ote. His track record of making rash decisions especially alarmed her when she was not in his immediate vicinity. She usually just dealt with the aftermath and humored his embellished tales of valor.

She wondered what tale was forthcoming now. Something about the damned grouper, she thought, "How might I be of service, Signore Pane?" she facetiously asked. She was ready for what she knew would be a harmless, playful exchange.

Ciro took a quick look around before touching just inside her khaki shorts and giving her gentle lips a kiss. "Oh I *so* needed that energizing boost," he whispered. "I'm still exhausted from that grouper!"

"Oh, of course, sir. But shouldn't I have loaned my energy to Ote instead?"

"It was a team effort. He came away from the fight unscathed, while look at me—battered!"

"Well, my battered boss, why is it that you seem to have so much energy and your scratches seem to be of no concern to you except when you need something? Don't you know that I have tasks to complete?"

"I am pained, yes, not by the deep wounds inflicted by a grouper, but by a girl who torments my heart with the seductive way she wipes down my dirty loungers!" Ciro answered with increasingly amused mock-aggrievement. "And yes, you take advantage of my weakness as you are a temptress determined to wreck my livelihood."

"All I can do is to keep the customers coming with my incredible good looks. If only we had a proper chef who might oblige their stomachs in the same way I oblige their eyes rather than a tawdry owner who likes to play with his *utensils* in the kitchen!"

"Your words cut like this knife. It's no wonder you are still without a diamond ring! Watch your tongue or you'll be wiping down my loungers the rest of your days!"

With another quick glance around, followed by an even quicker kiss, Ciro slapped Amalia's khakis, sending her on her way.

Amalia's job was secure regardless of her relationship with the owner. Tourists who stumbled upon the club by chance returned again and again, likely a direct result of her presence. For the last five years Ciro and Amalia had been seen holding hands, laughing, and occasionally nuzzling. As he watched her walk away, he hoped that they would never split, because working with her then would be a constant reminder of his undying love for her.

Amalia didn't get very far when her cell phone rang, the Radiohead ringtone indicating that it was Ote on the line.

"A-MA-LI-A!"

"OoooTAY!"

"I've been trying to reach Ciro but he's not picking up his phone."

"Why, we were just talking about you, Ote. Ciro told me he had to save you from a ferocious fish last night and in your clumsiness you knocked him into the sea with his cell phone in his pocket. Now he can't afford to marry me because he has to spend his money on a new phone."

Laughing, Ote continued the banter. "I wasn't even with him last night. I saw him out with a beautiful American tourist. One of those wild ones, though I'm sure it was all in good innocence."

"You have broken my heart for the last time, Ciro!" she said to her boyfriend with a smile that did not match her tone. "I will never speak to you again! Here, take this awful work shirt and give it to your new American girlfriend!" She smacked the phone, hoping it sounded like the phone being hurled at Ciro. She then rapidly tapped her perfectly manicured nails onto the phone's mouthpiece, simulating the sound of the phone sliding across the concrete. Handing the phone to Ciro, she whirled around to return to her work, skipping back to the few loungers that were still dirty. "What have you told her, Ote? She's furious!"

"Nice try, but no one can fool me. You'd think you two would have realized this by now. But enough of the silliness— can you talk?"

"No, I haven't seen Luigi today. Why what's up?"

Ote understood that the answer indicated that Ciro could listen but he couldn't really talk.

"I just dropped off some people in Positano, and on our way over I saw some kids playing by the entrance to the Africana!"

"You should swing by here on your way back and pick me up," Ciro blithely answered. "I need to grab a few things from Salvatore."

Ciro had about three more minutes to prep his tomatoes before Ote came zipping up in his low-slung white skiff. Ciro put down his knife and gave Amalia a quick caress of her shoulder, but not quick enough for Ote.

"Hey, Ote," Amalia called out. "Ciro told me about your

sick bedroom games. He even tried to get me to role-play with him—thank God he fell asleep! And I thought Juliana was an angel!"

"She *is* an angel, unlike your idiot boyfriend! But I'd be happy to give you a few private bedroom lessons if that's what you're asking!"

Blushing and pissed, Ote throttled down and rooster-tailed toward the Africana just as Ciro's first foot landed on the boat.

"Did you recognize them?" Ciro calmly asked.

"Well, they took me by surprise, as no one ever goes near there now, but I didn't want to slow down with passengers aboard."

"What were they doing? Could they have been fishing?"

"They were too close to the entrance; that's all I know."

Ote trimmed the motor to maximum speed, bouncing across the small waves. It was nearly impossible to be heard without screaming.

"Relax, Ote. Slow down man, we don't even know what's in the disk. Might offer nothing except yada, yada, yada. If it's discovered, who cares? No one knows that it was us who stashed it there. You know that kids play around there a lot."

Ote heard him but didn't slow his pace, nor did he feel relaxed being told something he already knew, even if he hadn't thought of it in this particular moment. As they skirted the last of the cliffs that blocked the view to the Africana, he shut down the engine and coasted to a stop.

The kids were kicking a soccer ball near the entrance to the Africana, specifically the entrance that was gated and chained closed. The other entrance, above the Africana's grotto, was accessible only by boat. These kids had a soccer ball, not a boat. They were also local kids they both knew, not yet teenagers.

"Ote, we must be patient until this evening. I'm also very much looking forward to discovering what we have found. If it's valuable we'll secure it in a safer location. In the meantime, don't let your mind play tricks on you. Now let's get out of here! I really do have to pick up a couple supplies and then get back to the kitchen. I actually have a real job, you know."

Ote frowned, unsatisfied. "I'm not even sure those are the same kids I saw earlier. What time do you want to meet tonight?"

"As planned, eight o'clock."

"I certainly hope you're not going to spend the hours apart sharing our conversations with everyone! You know I was kidding about Juliana, but then you share this joke with Amalia, and now she thinks I'm perverted!"

"Will you never relax, Ote? I didn't tell her anything—she was just trying to get you going! And can you blame me for trying to live a little like the King Ote, His Majesty of the Bedroom!"

Ote smiled. "I recall that every time—that's every time— we went out after a tourist, it was me, not you, who scored."

"That's why you are King Ote!"

"Whatever you do, my big-mouthed brother, don't mention to Amalia that Juliana has recently confided that she'd like to make it a threesome, sometime when you are away, when Amalia's all alone at our apartment getting just a little bit too drunk!"

"Yeah right, I can see Juliana now undressing in front of her! Make sure you edit yourself out of it before sharing the finer details."

With a last laugh, Ote started the engine and sped toward Praia.

Just before eight, they found themselves overlooking the sea through the La Praia tunnel. The effect was much like looking down a Manhattan street, one with colossal buildings on both sides, except here the endpoint was the sea and architects have yet to design a building that holds the fascination of Praiano's sea-hewn rocky walls.

Having arrived on time, Ciro would usually have had a chance to chat at length with his other friends as he waited for Ote. He did pause to say hello to an American couple he'd known forever, but even this brief stop had Ote, already at their table, drumming his fingers without almost any patience at all.

Ote had ordered a plate of spaghetti with anchovy sauce and a glass of the house white. In his desire to hurry, he had ordered for Ciro as well. In front of the empty chair sat a plate of grilled squid with zucchini spaghetti and a diet soda. Ciro rarely drank wine. His drink of choice was beer and anything but water.

"Todd and Angela said they're buying a place here!" Ciro said as he sat down.

"They may as well—they're here year after year. I wonder what he does for a living."

"I don't think he works. But Angela's told me of ten different jobs she's had over the years. I remember the first one, a chief of some kind."

"She's a doctor," Ote said with a proud grin. "That I know!"

"Please don't tell me how you know!"

Ote laughed. "I can tell you that I know. That's all!"

"To King Ote!"

Ote extended his curled hand, showcasing his wedding ring.

"I'll kiss your hand, kind king, if you're buying my meal tonight. But tell me more about your time with the doctor. Did you lure her with your magic smoke? Perhaps you had a wound to mend?"

"Question the king? How dare you? Would you prefer the garrote or the rack?"

"It will be off with *your* head, dear king, should Todd hear of your conquests!"

"He'd likely bow and thank me. Have you ever seen her

go off? The poor guy can't do anything right, especially before she's had her first glass of wine!"

This type of banter played out the entire meal, idiotic smiles awkwardly plastered on their faces. No mention of the disk was made, yet it consumed their thoughts. No one would have heard them anyway, seated outside on the terrace. Conversations there were subdued and inherently private.

After a delicious dinner that neither really tasted, they launched their boat in the direction of Positano. For an alibi, they had told anyone who would listen that they were visiting a friend at Music on the Rocks. Both agreed it was unlikely that anyone from Praiano would do the same.

They had dressed for the part too, wearing what was, at their age, their hippest wear. Daytime always found them in shorts or jeans. Ciro was in jeans, but of the decidedly less crumpled, less stained variety. He knew ahead of time he would be the one disassembling the disk. The white linen slacks Ote had chosen for the evening only confirmed that he had little intention of participating. Ciro never let on that he had figured out his friend thirty-five years ago, and he occasionally used his insights to his friendly advantage.

Once they turned the corner of La Praia, Ciro reached under his bench seat. "Look what I have here—Mr. Tool Kit!"

He held up his fully charged DeWalt electric socket and screwdriver with a complete case of sockets to fit virtually every fastener.

"That's great," Ote retorted in a tone that would have convinced most. "I was going remove all the screws with my old-fashioned screwdriver. I couldn't let you risk more injury to your hand. My God, you can barely walk … and every time you move your arm, your face contorts with—"

"That's why I brought this electric screwdriver for you to use," Ciro countered.

"It looks like it sprays grease everywhere! I can't use that in my white slacks!"

Ciro temporarily deserted his captain's seat and moved toward Ote with an evil grin, whirling the grease-spitting screwdriver.

"Does this scare the little girl, or does she like the grease?"

"Get back! You'll run the battery down!"

Within no time they arrived at the cave opening and just as quickly were out of the boat, feet practically bouncing as if they were children again. They knew it was likely at this hour that someone would see their boat moored at the Africana's neglected, but still functioning, entrance to the grotto. If the passerby was a local, they would most logically conclude the pair had stopped to smoke a joint.

Armed with the DeWalt, Ciro and Ote estimated that it would take five minutes to dismantle the disk. They continued to bet on what it contained. The one thing they agreed on is that it would hold a prize of great value.

Ote led the way with his flashlight, while followed the sound of the screwdrivers clattered in his loose white slacks.

"It's gone!" Ote howled. "The damn thing's gone!"

Ciro shuddered and then recognized his partner's playful tone.

"Get your light over here, Signore Gilligan!"

Then it was Ciro's turn to fire a "Damn!," except he meant his seriously. "The thing is fastened together with star screws! Who'd use star screws?"

"Aliens, I suppose," Ote said in a thoughtful voice.

"I have a star driver set, but it's back at my house. We'll have to walk up the stairs."

"Are you serious?" Ote sputtered. "Why not say we forgot something, boat back, and grab your car?"

"Let's walk it—we both could use the exercise and it's not that far. By the time we take the boat back, hike to the car, and fight the traffic, we won't have saved any time. It's more productive this way!"

"Productive? Any more all you talk about is productivity! How about we not sweat our butts off on this productive hike and be smart instead!"

"Ah, does the little girl worry about staining her nice clothes?" Ciro fired up his grease-sputtering drill, chasing Ote out of the cave.

They picked their way back across the grotto to the rocky steps that led up into the now-vacant, mostly dark main floor of the club and squeezed through the gate at the top that barely accommodated their size. Ote looked down at his linen pants and was relieved to see they hadn't torn.

From there, the hike up began with a series of steep zigzag pedestrian ramps. After nearly half a mile, the ramps gave way to 388 irregular rocky steps to Ciro's little apartment.

Around the 151st step, Ote decided to start taking the steps two at a time, then moving into a light jog. The race was on, for Ciro was never one to be left behind by his oldest friend.

They had stopped twice along their way to this point, initially on the pretext that they needed to discuss a new plan. The second time, the two wheezing middle-aged men admitted they needed an honest stop to rest. Now they were nearly running at top speed to finish the remaining two hundred steps. Determined to win the race both ignored what their bodies were screaming at them.

Ciro retained his race crown when Ote stopped about thirty steps short of the finish line. Buckled over with hands on his knees, he wondered why he ever started this ridiculous race. He was too exhausted to even begin to figure it out.

Five minutes later Ciro hopped out of his apartment, having replaced his drenched shirt, though he continued to sweat in the fresh one too. He carried two bottles of water and his star driver set, which he held up triumphantly.

He tossed Ote one bottle of water, keeping the other for himself. They headed back down the steps, thirty minutes delayed from their original schedule.

"I thought I had you," Ote gasped, still out of breath, "right before I felt like my heart might explode. And I thought you could barely walk, after all that moping about your shin!"

"I could tolerate the pain in my crushed leg, but not the pain of listening to you brag."

"Well, it wasn't even a race. I was just trying to increase our productivity, as you always say! Had it been an official race you can be sure I wouldn't have quit."

Whatever time they gained by their race was lost on the way back down, as both needed rest for a breather at virtually every bend, mostly to hack up blackened smoky mucus. Ote evened the score for the day by declaring he had broken the world record for mucus expectorated in an evening—indeed, he really was really quite proud of it.

Huffing and puffing with hearts still pounding, they crept back into the pitch-black grotto, now an hour behind schedule. Ote did not make it unscathed past the chained gate this time, snagging a linen pant and tearing a rip in the shape of an "L" midway up his thigh. He shrugged and passed it off as a trivial price to pay for the mountain of gold that awaited them inside the disk.

Ote held the flashlight while Ciro began his assault on the smaller disk atop the larger body. Ote's flashlight shook with the excitement he could not contain.

The sound of the screwdriver was amplified by the rocky walls. Ote remarked that the reverberations sounded more like a DJ Tiesto concert. But in minutes, Ciro had removed all of the star screws from the top disk.

Then he used his flathead screwdriver to pry around the upper, smaller disk's edges, finally uncovering what appeared to be a mini-computer, battery, and small cylindrical tank.

"So it *is* a bomb," Ote whispered, taking a step back.

"Hold that flashlight steady and don't be a baby."

Neither had any experience with submersible electronics

but the wiring struck them as very well manicured. A pneumatic hose ran from the tank into the larger disk through a tightly fitted, dual-chambered port. The two men shared an ominous feeling, though neither of them expressed it.

"I hope there's something better in the larger disk," Ote grumbled. "Look at my pants—they're ruined. And for what—a fancy submarine that does me no good?"

"Let's see if this fancy submarine has any valuables aboard! Since your pants are already ruined, perhaps you'd like to take your turn on the bottom disk?"

"Juliana might be able to repair the hole but she could never get that grease out!"

So Ciro set the small disk aside and began to unfasten the first of the fifty or so star screws that encircled the larger disk. It took longer than he anticipated, more than five minutes, but eventually the final star screw joined the pile in a cranny of the rock floor.

Ciro again used his flathead screwdriver as a crowbar, but this time the top would not budge. Ciro inspected around the disk's entire band and found two screws he had missed in his haste, though he chose to blame Ote's shaking hand instead.

"Hand me the electric again!" he ordered, and Ote quickly complied. Ciro removed the missed screws and loosened the seal with his flathead.

Ciro stood from his kneeled position and tested the weight of the top. Weirdly enough, it wasn't very heavy. It seemed the components of the smaller disk comprised most of the entire weight.

"To our wealth, dear friend!"

This was the best toast Ciro had managed to compose, despite his efforts throughout the entire day to devise something more profound, something along the lines of Armstrong's "One small step for man, one giant leap for mankind."

And with that, he hoisted the top off in much the same

manner as the chef at a Michelin three-star restaurant reveals his Dover sole.

The light went out at that exact moment. "The flashlight—it's broke!" Ote cried. Then with a laugh, he flipped the flashlight back on to illuminate the now-topless disk.

"Holy crap!" Ote exhaled.

Both were stunned, literally unable to believe their eyes. Ciro tossed the oversized, remarkably weightless top to the side. It clamored against the rocks. He had forgotten he was holding it despite the pain that was swelling in his hand and elbow. Subconsciously he attributed the pain to his injuries from last night.

Ote and Ciro high-fived, both talking simultaneously, neither really hearing the other. Then, as if DJ Funky Soul were there cranking up the volume, they both began a wild whirling, their dance of a lifetime, blazing like a spasm from the sun. Ote's dance gave the flashlight in his hand the effect of a strobe light, intermittently showcasing one dancer and then the other. He was beyond elation.

Then the strobe focused on Ciro, who was hunched over and violently eliminating the squid and pasta that formerly resided in his stomach. He rose abruptly, grabbed Ote with a frightened look, and pushed him back toward their boat. "I need some fresh air!" he said weakly.

Ote noticed the fear in his dear friend's eyes and voice. As they neared the rocky exit, Ote saw that Ciro had turned an ashen pale. Beads of sweat were running down his forehead.

"Are you all right?"

Ciro didn't answer, but his terrified eyes conveyed the dread he couldn't voice. Ote recognized it well, as his father had died in front of him just before Christmas last year. With a final limp high-five, Ciro stumbled to his left, regained his balance for a moment, then fell backward into his friend's arms. He seemed to want to try to stand on his own, but with each desperate, failed attempt, the fear in his eyes was magnified.

Ote carried his collapsed comrade through the grotto to where their boat was docked some thirty feet away. He gently laid Ciro in the boat, started the motor, and hammered the throttle. Terrified, he cried and shook uncontrollably. Suddenly, he was alone in a real race—a race to save the life of his dear friend.

Eliciting all of the saints to hear his prayers for Ciro, Ote rounded the towering walled entrance to La Praia and aimed the speeding boat at an opening on the beach, the throttle still hot. He crashed ashore, bouncing and skipping nearly twenty feet across the rocks. The motor's prop flew high into the air and somersaulted across the beach.

"*Aiuto, mi aiuti per favore, amico mio, aiutare!*"

Ote was screaming, pleading for help from anyone within earshot. Tourists dining near the beach, who had witnessed the insane entry onto the shore, ran from their tables to assist the Italian. Most hadn't comprehended a word of what he'd shrieked, but his desperation was universally understood.

Chapter 3: Ever Waxing

Amalia had arrived at Praia just moments after Ciro and Ote left. She had plans to meet her younger sister, Francesca. Both looked stunning in skimpy miniskirts paired with cropped tank tops exposing their slim, inviting midriffs. She had hoped to catch Ciro before he left and was disappointed to have missed him, longing for one last hug. They always expressed their love for one another openly and without pretense.

From Amalia's perspective, Ciro's behavior that day was strange. He'd shown up bleeding with bruises on his elbow and shin. He had stuck with his claim that he'd been clumsy, though she could tell that he had a secret that he very much wished to share. She had cleaned the wound on his hand and wrapped it with gauze. Despite his injuries, he seemed more upbeat than usual. He smiled at her as he lightly brushed her arm and shoulder. Not in the way one would normally act after just having their heart and pride broken by a grouper.

Amalia and Francesca ordered rum and Cokes and margarita pizza at the little bar on the beach. Over drinks and dinner, they discussed Francesca's new boyfriend, a tourist from Rome.

"I'm jealous—he's hot! Those abs!"

"Yeah, but only wants one thing—and you can guess what that is. Too bad Ciro doesn't have a brother—I need someone from here, not Rome. But who knows, maybe he'll fall in love with me and leave his breathtaking Rome."

"Maybe he'll take *your* breath away and move you to his dirty Rome!"

Francesca giggled. "He's one of those guys who wear baggy swim trunks. You know what that means, don't you!"

"Maybe that he's humbly hung?"

"Ciro wears the baggy type! His are even flowered pink!"

"He needs the extra room!"

After more laughs and talk of boyfriends, they finished their pizza and ordered a second round of rum and Cokes. As she sipped her drink, Amalia saw that Todd was sitting at a table in the corner. She thought he was attractive for an older guy, and often teased Ciro that she had her sights on the wealthy American. He was about six-foot-two and a solidly built with blue eyes and graying brown hair that was always cut short. He had been vacationing here for years and was a frequent sun lounger at One Fire. His wife was with him, but Amalia couldn't remember her name … Was it Annabelle?

For his part, Todd had noticed Amalia the second she and her sister had made their entrance at La Praia. The two were impossible not to notice. He had already paid his bill and was preparing to take a water taxi back to Positano, but Amalia's arrival spurred him to order one last bottle of Furore, a tasty local red wine. It didn't take much effort to convince his wife, Angela, to enjoy another bottle and continue taking in the idyllic setting.

Todd's pose was laid back, his legs outstretched, ankles crossed and hands clasped behind his head. He was pleased when he saw Amalia heading in his direction with a shy wave and smile. The Furore tasted better than ever—a wise investment, he concluded.

"Good to see you, Todd! Did you have nice dinner?" Amalia's broken English only accentuated her sexiness.

Angela, who'd had her back to the sisters, had noticed that something was arresting her husband's attention. She was about to scold him when a speeding boat turned frantically into the harbor and crashed ashore.

"Good God!" was Angela's immediate diagnosis. She sprang quickly to her feet, her instinct to aid instinctively kicking in. She nearly knocked Amalia to the ground as she bolted up from her chair. Amalia watched paralyzed, her jaw dropped in astonishment. Amalia knew the boat, and she understood Ote's pleas very well.

By the time Angela reached the scene, Ciro had already been removed from the boat and was lying as white and motionless as the moon. For the first time in twenty years in Praiano, she overtly declared her profession and ferociously ordered those surrounding Ciro to give the man room to breathe.

She dropped quickly to her knees to check Ciro's pulse and breathing. Once she established that he was in cardiac arrest, she immediately began CPR. She didn't pause to acknowledge that the man was her friend. In these crises, they were always just patients. Emotions were not allowed to cloud her vision.

"Is there a defibrillator here?"

She knew the answer even before asking. Of course there wasn't. She also knew that the nearest hospital was in Amalfi some fifteen kilometers away. Had anyone called an ambulance, she wondered, mostly to herself, as she continued plunging her palms into Ciro's chest. His eyes were wide open, his face gaunt, and he remained unresponsive.

By then Amalia had torn herself from her shock and rushed to the scene. Sobbing, she threw herself onto Ciro. Francesca did the same. Todd was able to coax them off in his best Italian so that his wife could continue the CPR. The two sisters huddled and hugged Ote as Todd took over the breathing for Ciro while his wife continued compressing his heart.

"I've got a pulse!" Angela declared a few minutes later. Sweat was pouring down her face. "Slight, but it's a pulse."

The English-speaking tourists reacted with joy, the tone of their cheers serving as the necessary translation to the Germans, Norwegians, and Italians, who then understood the optimistic turn.

Salvatore Pisacane had already ordered his Mercedes to

the nearest accessible spot. He wondered who he should have drive it when he spotted Nello, a local SITA bus driver who had navigated the treacherous coastal highway for more than thirty years. Salvatore commanded him to abandon his dinner and assume the driver's seat of the Benz, their impromptu ambulance.

They rolled Ciro, still unconscious but breathing, onto a tablecloth and rushed him to the waiting Mercedes. Angela squeezed into the back with her patient and ordered Amalia out of the front seat in lieu of her husband, a former emergency room RN.

A local named Antonio quickly ushered Amalia, Francesca, and Ote into his Renault. They were all friends, and given the nature of Praiano, probably distant cousins.

They followed the flying Mercedes, the horns of both cars blaring, their lights flashing. After the first mile, neither the four-cylinder Renault nor its driver could keep pace with the ambulance. About halfway to the hospital, a local policeman joined the pursuit. He trailed farther and farther behind before finally ending his efforts. Those in front of him were driving at a mad pace and he wasn't going to die along with them in an effort to catch up.

Ciro reached the hospital in an astonishing ten minutes after speeding the fifteen kilometers along the sinister, serpentine coastal road. Those few cars and scooters they had encountered quickly became a blur behind them. The Benz never even slowed to pass. There were several close calls but Nello, who knew every bend along the way, remained calm for the entire trip. Though confident in his driving, Nello was not as confident about Ciro's future.

When Amalia, Francesca, and Ote arrived several minutes behind the ambulance, Ciro has already been admitted to the emergency room. With anxiety throbbing through every vein, they waited for news of their friend's fate.

Chapter 4: You Are Malevolent

Two years before the great grouper fiasco, the strange disk, and Ciro's heart attack, Alessio Bianco had been summoned by his cell phone. Whenever his second line rang, he knew it was important and always answered.

"*Pronto*," he responded. "*Sì … sì … sì.*" In less than a minute he understood his task. The caller was a man he had never met. Every month for the last ten years, since he had been recruited—or rather, dragooned—€10,000 was deposited into his banking account by his unknown employer. His specific value was that he had sources. And with this phone call from the faceless man, he would again make happen what was demanded of him.

At thirty-seven years old, Alessio was an avid tennis player. When this particular call came in, he was on his way to board the underground train, Roma Metropolitana, to the Tennis Club Lanciani, one of Rome's finest tennis clubs. Alessio was one of Rome's finest players. But he turned around as instructed and went home to wait for the parcel, which was always delivered by a special messenger.

He fronted as a real estate broker, though he never spent much time maintaining the guise. In fact, he was very much a struggling real estate agent before he had been hired by his unknown employers. In those lean days he played tennis on Rome's public courts.

He never knew when the second line might ring. It had sat dormant for up to five months at one point, but the deposits always found their way into his account. The calls only worked one direction, the unknown caller contacting him but never vice versa. They never lasted more than a minute and his job was to listen, confirm with a "*Sì?*" and perform the task.

Though he never actually performed any of the tasks, he had sources, and his sources had sources. He was more of a task launcher than performer. His job was to get the *pallino* bouncing. That's how he thought of it, anyway. Somehow he had successfully vanquished the ghastly memories of his times as a performer.

Usually he made his calls from his San Lorenzo district apartment near the Termini train station and La Sapienza, the oldest and largest university in Europe. This was Rome's most vibrant area, where bars, dance clubs, coffee shops, restaurants, pizzerias, and *trattorias* lined the street level of three- and four-story brick and stone buildings.

Alessio lived on the second floor of a four-story red brick building. He was a rarity in that he owned his home. He was sprawled atop his silver-blue davenport and staring in a daze through the large window overlooking Via dei Volsci when he was abruptly interrupted by his intercom.

Startled, he vaulted to his feet, ran down the marble stairs to the street, and accepted the meter-long cardboard shipping tube from a courier astride an idling Vespa. It was never the same courier and this was the first time a tube was delivered.

He marched back upstairs, popped off the CD-sized blue lid, and removed the contents—a series of five blueprints, each with a different perspective.

The materials for its construction were specified. Whatever it was, it was to be mostly constructed of a hi-tech ceramic, the type that was used for the engine components of an F-16 fighter. Noted for its lightweight composition, strength, and heat-resistant properties, this hi-tech ceramic was the most expensive material synthesized. Yet to his novice eye it appeared to be intended for some kind of shipping container.

Without losing a moment on further thought, he knew who to call because *they* knew who to call. Within the hour Alessio was on his way to the airport with a destination to Jamnagar, India, a city on the Arabian Sea and home to

Havikiran Ceramic. After four years of doors opening for him, the lightning speed of the routine no longer amazed him. Now it was expected.

There were no direct flights from Rome to Jamnagar. This would be an arduous trip but one he would only have to make once, so he believed. He would remain there through the project completion and delivery. He connected first in Istanbul and then Mumbai. After an exhausting trip of more than twenty hours, he wondered how those who flew economy survived in their cramped, upright confines.

An attractive twenty-something woman, petite with straight black hair flowing several inches below her dainty shoulders, was waiting for him at the exit from the security area. She didn't have a sign with his name on it, but she seemed to recognize him instantly. She was the only woman awaiting arrivals; all the others were men forming a sea of knee-length bleached white tops with matching pants.

She was wearing a long dress, its silk resplendent in various shades of floral green. She stood out from the crowd as Alessio must have in his sky-blue Prada suit, the linen now wrinkled from the trials of multiple flights. His pink Brioni dress shirt was in a similarly distressed state.

"I trust you had a good flight, Signore Bianco," she said in slightly stilted Italian. "My name is Aprajita Shridhar. We will stop off at your hotel so that you might freshen up before I take you to our facility."

Aprajita provoked illicit thoughts. Her ability to speak basic Italian was the most obvious reason Havikiran had delegated her. They quickly deferred to speaking English, which they both were—by and large—fluent in. Alessio liked her, her accent, and he wondered how she looked without her dress. He already found himself hoping he would have the opportunity to investigate. With thoughts already drifting toward James Bond-esque escapades, he lost no time in integrating this beautiful Indian girl as the female lead in his evolving fantasy.

He lamented what felt like a too short trip to his hotel. The time in the car was long enough, however, for him to become intoxicated with her scent.

"Have you been to India before, Mr. Bianco?"

"Never, but I think I love the place already! What's that round building over there?"

"That's our governmental office. They just finished it … let me think … oh, back in November of last year. Some famous Italian architect designed it. It was very controversial at first."

"That would make sense—it looks like that's an obelisk centered on top."

"What is it you call it?"

"An obelisk—it's a Roman thing!"

"There's your hotel, Mr. Bianco. Fort Chanwa. It was converted into a hotel many years ago."

It was four stories tall, built in the same red sandstone as many of the surrounding structures. The grounds were obviously inspired by English gardens, and there was a large circular drive up to the entrance. Inside he found an elegant lobby dominated by white marble and accented with black marble. He found his suite to be equally appealing. As Aprajita waited for him in the lobby, he took a quick shower, put on fresh clothes, and returned to the lobby, his hair still damp.

"So refreshing, Aprajita!"

She smiled, pleased that he had pronounced her name just right. "You're all the talk at the facility—they seem very anxious to meet you!"

"I won't have much to do," he modestly replied. "I'm just delivering these plans so you can build something for the company I work for. It's a pretty easy job for me, but very complex for you, which is why I'm here. Very few places in the world could build it."

"Most of our projects are of that nature, but I don't know

any of the details. Few do, and certainly not someone with my rank. I mostly just make sure that the customers are happy!"

Alessio smiled, though he would have preferred her to be more coy. It was more fun to chase than catch them at the starting line.

At the offices of Havikiran Ceramic, Alessio was greeted by Dr. Romil Bahl. Romil was short in stature, just a bit pudgy, and had perfectly groomed black hair. He was dressed sharply, though conservatively, in a dark tailored suit. He was about fifty years old and seemed wary of this project that had seemingly emerged from obscurity.

"So good to meet you, Mr. Bianco. I hope we can meet your expectations!"

"Here are the plans, Dr. Bahl. I'm confident you will meet my company's expectations. I'll give you a day to review them."

Alessio noticed that Romil's English was more American than British. He noticed that the diploma in Ceramic Engineering on the wall was from the University of Buffalo.

"Mr. Bianco, if you wish, we might begin with a quick tour of our facilities?"

Alessio answered by tacitly ignoring the question. "If you could have that information by this time tomorrow, I'd appreciate it."

Romil looked visibly stunned. "Yes, of course, Mr. Bianco."

"Like you, Dr. Bahl, I have people that I report to. I don't know what type of preparations have been made, but it's vital that we move forward immediately. Silly tours don't advance our mission. I trust the facilities are perfectly suited for the manufacturing of this design."

"Of course you are correct, Mr. Bianco. We'll meet back here tomorrow. If you'll excuse me, I'll return to my perfectly suited office and begin immediately!"

Aprajita smiled at Alessio as he stepped out of Romil's

office. "Looks like you're stuck with me, Mr. Bianco. Did you and Romil hit it off?"

"I was very pleased with the meeting. Romil's very bright—a very sharp man and a real clothes hound too!" His smile that accompanied this statement was genuine, though generated by Aprajita's beauty rather than Romil's fashion sense.

"He is our best! And the nicest guy! He heads our charity to help pull our people from poverty. If you wish for me to join you for dinner this evening, it would be my pleasure."

"I'd love to have dinner with you. At my hotel?"

"Yes. I will drop you off and meet you back at the hotel restaurant at … oh let's say eight o'clock?

"Perfect—see you then!"

That evening the two enjoyed a delicious meal of Gujarati cuisine—*kadhi* for her and *dal dhokli* for him—coupled with a relatively innocent evening of conversation. Alessio's thoughts, however, were not so innocent, and he had a difficult time concentrating as she listed all the things he might see while he was in the city. That night he dreamt of Aprajita and woke with a renewed determination to make her his lover for the duration of his stay.

When he returned to Havikiran that afternoon, Romil made his report brief and to the point. Alessio sensed that the man didn't like him but he didn't much care. "If we construct three vessels, the cost will be ten millions rupees plus a onetime set-up fee of one million rupees." Converted to Euro this was nearly €500,000.

"Let's make it twenty million rupees," Alessio blandly replied. "It's important I have one within two weeks for testing. If the testing goes as planned, the project should be complete within the month."

Alessio was not asking. He entirely indulged the authority his position brought him, even though he had no clue what justified that authority.

Romil didn't question the ludicrous deadline. He had no choice but to meet it. The owner of Havikiran Ceramic, who he had never met before, had called him into his office to insist that this project be given top priority. Everything else, even their military contracts, would have to wait.

"I'll need a retainer of twenty-five percent of the total project," said Romil, "with the balance due upon completion."

"Not a problem," Alessio replied, standing up to take his leave. "Full payment had already been made." It had been deposited into Havikiran's account in the same untraceable manner as Alessio's monthly remuneration.

Romil's first day had been wasted. Upon examining the plans he had immediately went to his superior, Gautam Sircar, with grave concerns.

"Why would the client not design redundancies for the main component? There's room for a signal strength that would signal them within five miles of the disk at any depth and we have room for two, should the main fail. The receiver is even smaller than the one in their design, the size of a large cell phone. You can get one off the shelf at Raytheon for a hundred thousand rupees!"

Gautam was usually a very reasonable man who, under most circumstances, would instantly concur with Romil's sound concerns, but this time he had other issues to deal with. He was courteous, though unusually curt, and quickly decided with a shrug of his shoulders.

"We weren't hired to design this thing, just to build it. I don't like this project anyway and don't want to have any knowledge of it again. This came from above me, so please do as they ask!"

"With all due respect, I believe it's my duty to inform the client that as designed this system has a glaring flaw. It's a difficult environment, the ocean depths. It doesn't make sense and can be corrected with little extra cost. I must tell you that my design analysis report will include these grave concerns. It's simply not prudent to move into production without addressing this issue!"

Gautam scowled. "I said I don't like it. Have you ever seen a project placed on the faster track than this one? We've stopped military production for this project! Just do your job!"

"I have made my concerns known," Romil replied. "I'll not concern you with any of the other details that we usually confer on and I appreciate your guidance. If you'll excuse me, I need to meet with Purchasing to arrange for the immediate shipping of the vendor components." He stood up and left Gautam's office without waiting for a reply.

Alessio spent the next ten days escaping Jamnagar, as Aprajita seemed eager to whisk him away on day trips. There wasn't much to see in the city, which was known for containing the largest oil refinery in the world, which polluted the air with a rancid, crude smell. He did enjoy a visit to the Bala Hanuman Temple, where the mantra "*Sri Ram, Jai Ram, Jai Jai Ram*" has been chanted unabated for nearly fifty years. His time spent with Aprajita only fostered his sexual appetite for her. Back in Rome, he was known to date a wide variety of beautiful, always younger, women.

For now, he was playing tennis with a local pro, a match arranged by Aprajita. For Alessio, bashing the ball about was always therapeutic, physically and mentally. He was up four-love in the first set his phone rang. Though it was only on line one, he stopped play to answer the call.

Romil had good news to report: the prototype was complete and ready for testing. He had abandoned his wife and their two teenage boys for the last ten days, sleeping in his office and working nearly around the clock. The technicians building the underwater storage disk worked twelve-hour shifts. Seven men worked the day shift while four others continued the work through the night.

Alessio sensed the pride in Romil's voice. The engineer's furious pace was stealing valuable time from Alessio's top priority. He would have to adjust his schedule accordingly. He was known to always get the job done, whatever it was. Aprajita would be no different.

After dispatching the local tennis pro, Alessio returned to his hotel, showered, lunched, and arrived at Havikiran just before three. He was led to a glass holding tank some sixty feet tall. A crane lifted the prototype and dropped it into the water with a splash. Within seconds, it sank to the bottom of the tank.

"I wrote the program instructions myself," said Romil. "If it's working properly, it will release in one hour."

They retired to Romil's office. For the first time Alessio noticed the tennis trophies and plaques that decorated the wall behind Romil's desk. This prompted a nearly hour-long discussion, focusing first on the French Open then underway in Paris, followed by stories dating back to Vijay Amritraj and Leander Paes. Romil was especially enthusiastic about the state of his son's game, who he touted as the next Ramesh Krishnan. They would have missed the test if Romil's secretary hadn't interrupted them.

They hurried back to the test plant aboard a golf cart and arrived with two minutes to spare. Romil was uncharacteristically anxious as the final seconds ticked down. But at precisely the right moment, the bolts fitted to the leaden anchor exploded, releasing the disk. At the same time, a Kevlar float encircling the disk inflated, propelling its ascent.

"Are you receiving the signal?" Romil asked a nearby technician, who nodded in assent. Then he turned to Alessio. "We'll wait for two days and continually monitor the system. I'll call you if we have any issues—otherwise I'll see you back here for the open water tests."

While in the storage tank, the disk's system worked as designed, delighting the engineers on the project. When they removed the lid to the disk, the seal had successfully kept any water out of the interior despite pressures to simulate the sea at six hundred meters, and the 226.42 pounds specified for the cargo hull easily lifted to the surface as designed.

A few mornings later, Alessio and Romil met aboard the yacht *Purpose Driven*. Since the first test, the anchor system, the computer, and the seals had been restored to launch conditions. During the two-hour trip out to sea to reach the proper testing depth, the two men drifted back to their shared love of tennis.

They mostly discussed yesterday's exciting five-set men's semifinal at Roland Garros. Federer's victory had especially pleased Alessio, who loved the one-handed backhand and lamented its growing disappearance from the game.

"He played with purpose, he was committed to his game plan and he stuck with it! That Argentine, what a crybaby!"

"Mr. Nice Guy, he's the pampered baby! That match was Portro's in three sets if they hadn't fixed the tiebreaker!"

"They may have missed that call," Alessio admitted, "but you can't just fall into the tank. Think of it as a learning experience for your sons. Attack your opponents' weaknesses relentlessly!"

Alessio quickly regretted mentioning Romil's sons and tennis in the same sentence. For the next ninety minutes Romil droned on and on about his sons' tennis games. Apparently they had each recently won their respective singles titles at a large regional tournament. Much to Alessio's dismay, their father had watched every point and was eager to recount each one. Alessio nearly wept with relief when a technician interrupted to announce the next test.

Again the disk was dropped, again with precisely 226.42 pounds of cargo. While it descended, Romil could have easily resumed his interminable recap, so Alessio claimed seasickness and was led to a bunk belowdecks. He told the valet to wake him a few minutes before the disk was set to surface.

About four hours later, Alessio was leaning over the railing and watching the disk surface with the same precision as the first controlled test. It emitted its signature ping as it emerged just less than a quarter-mile from where it had been dropped. They removed it from the water as quickly as possible, for they couldn't afford to have it discovered. By design, it was colored to blend into the sea.

There was ample time on the return trip to conduct the post-test analysis, which the system passed with flying colors. They arrived back into port in the early evening, the sun still blazing but beginning its westward descent.

"Your work has been exemplary and I fear my time here is nearing an end," said Alessio. "On behalf of my superiors, I want to express our gratitude. And we should try to get out onto the tennis court before I leave!"

"I'm pleased the project is nearing completion," Romil replied. "It's been a very difficult time away from my family and with other project deadlines near, it seems unlikely that I'll have the opportunity to play tennis with you."

That was fine with Alessio. "I understand. Few want to compete against me on the tennis court—just ask your local pro!"

With that the two men separated with a promise to meet one last time at Romil's facility to provide delivery and instructions. As Alessio was led to his car, he checked his watch and was pleased to see he wouldn't be late for his dinner date with Aprajita.

At the hotel he dressed in his finest clothes, stone-hued Prada linen slacks and a long-sleeved black linen shirt with the top buttons opened. He splashed liberally with Light Blue, a D&G fragrance he had been saving specifically for this capture.

Aprajita picked him up at eight as planned. She was wearing a more revealing dress than she had on previous evenings—black silk, simple and low cut. It hugged her body, emphasizing her toned, slender legs. He speculated that she too had a plan. They were heading to the town's premier Italian-inspired restaurant, which he had been saving for this night.

"Well, you certainly seem very spry this evening," she said. "Even your fragrance is rather vibrant! You must be excited that the project is nearly complete and you'll get to return home."

"It's this evening with you that inspires my smile!"

"Finally tired of me, are you? Relieved to see the light at the end of the tunnel!"

"Who could possibly tire of you? You've been so very kind with your time—the consummate hostess!"

"We've had a lot of laughs, that's for sure. Remember that crazy man at Shah's Temple? I think you may have saved my life that day!"

"I've always pictured myself as a knight in shining armor! Let's make this night very special—not as a good-bye, that won't do. Let's really celebrate!"

At the restaurant he ordered a bottle of Cristal, the best champagne the restaurant could provide. He convinced himself that she was smiling more, was deliberately throwing sparks his way. On none of their previous dinners had she joined him in a drink. Now she was on her third glass of the bubbly before they had finished their calamari.

Meanwhile Romil was just finishing dinner with his wife, Shalini, his sons, Guhan and Vijay, and his parents, who lived only a three-minute walk from his home. They were a very close family. Romil's three siblings, two sisters and a brother, were all doctors of the medical variety who lived in the States, but they all gathered at Romil's parent's beachfront estate in Goa for Diwali every year.

It was always quite a gathering—and a growing one, as his sister had just recently announced the good news that her family was expecting a third child. During much of dinner, the discussion focused on this annual pilgrimage, which would take place in a few short months.

After dinner they retreated to the rear terrace, surrounded

by a kidney-shaped pool. The blue glow from the water was their only light. Grandpa Bahl excused himself to go the bathroom. As he wound around the pool, he stepped on one of his grandson's errant tennis balls and fell to the ground with a thump.

"Father, Father, are you alright?" Romil cried as he rushed over. His first fear was a heart attack, but he saw that his father seemed to be laughing it off.

"I'm fine. Just a little turn to my ankle. I stepped on something, not sure what. Help me up, please."

"Yes, of course, Father."

By now they had all gathered around the fallen man. Romil's mother blamed the two glasses of wine her husband had with dinner. "Too much to drink, my dear?"

"Not yet, but some whiskey would help prevent swelling in this ankle!"

Romil's father allowed his son to assist him to the bathroom. This injury created a problem for Romil. His father was set to be his partner in a doubles match the next morning against the boys. He resolved to call the Italian. If his game was half as good as he crowed, the boys would find tomorrow's match quite taxing.

The next morning, Aprajita awoke amid the luxurious comfort of the Fort Chanwa hotel, stirred by Alessio, who was preparing to meet the Bahls at the local tennis club. The previous night had been a fulfillment of previously unacknowledged desires, an exploration and a learning experience for her, entirely unrelated to love. Inside she was glowing, remorse occupying no crevice of her mind. She was slightly, though pleasantly, unsettled to find herself hoping for more instruction.

"Ah, you have awoken, my sweet Aprajita!"

"Must you leave? Come back to bed and spend the day with me!"

She drew the silken sheets down slightly, her dark eyes

wide and inviting, lips slightly parted seductively to tempt him further.

"Nothing would provide me more joy. But rather unluckily, I will be spending the entire day with Romil's family, but I promise to call you as soon as I can escape. We're going to his home for lunch after the tennis match—maybe you would care to join us?"

"I don't think that's a great idea. I hope he doesn't notice my car in the parking lot. I doubt my employers will approve of this extra attention that I've given you!"

Alessio leapt into the bed, unable to resist a minute or two of cuddling. He couldn't imagine tolerating a day with Romil and his sons, of whom he had already heard more than he could stand. He tried to find comfort in the hope that Mrs. Bahl might at least provide some visual stimulation.

"I must be going, but my thoughts will be with you until this evening. Now wish me luck on the court."

Alessio was the master manipulator; he was utterly convincing no matter what mask he chose for his guise. His relationship with Aprajita was purely physical, and he had no qualms in saying whatever was necessary to facilitate the continued satisfaction of his erotic desires.

"Good luck, Alessio. If you win, I just might have a surprise for you this evening."

He met Romil in the hotel lobby. Both men were both dressed in Wimbledon white. Alessio smirked inwardly when he noticed that Romil had parked right next to Aprajita's BMW (or more likely, he thought, Havikiran's BMW). Memories of last night's recent conquest relaxed his mind, and as he thought of Aprajita's naked curves, he lightly stroked her car's bumper. Then he saw Romil's sons in the back of his SUV and didn't bother to hide a sullen pout. But vengeance, he consoled himself, would soon be his on the court. That they were children made no difference.

"Very wise, Romil, to play in early morning," Alessio said

as he climbed into the car. "Much better conditions than hitting with that pro mid-afternoon! Don't get me wrong, I love to sweat but that heat was intolerable!"

Vijay, the older of the two sons and the one who should have known better, decided to talk some smack. "Excuse me, Mr. Bianco, but the heat you experienced that afternoon will be chilly compared to the heat my brother and I will make you endure!"

Alessio laughed, but Romil was feigned mortification. "Vijay, sportsmanship is what tennis is truly about. Ah, the youth of today, Alessio. Now let's go pound sportsmanship up their you-know-whats."

Alessio hoped he wouldn't puke!

As they warmed up it was quickly clear that Alessio was the best player on the court. His fluid form, crisp strikes, and relaxed confidence were clearly evident. Romil was clearly the worst, but still a very advanced player.

The children were very skilled for their age, both with formidable backhands—though two-handed, Alessio was sorry to see. Their forehands were equally solid, crushing topspin naturally, but their serves revealed their youthful inexperience and they lacked the ability to discern their opponents' weaknesses. Such discernment, and subsequent exploitation, was Alessio's preeminent strength.

In the end, the teenagers could not overcome the power and experience of their opponents. They lost two and two, but the match was closer than the score indicated.

As planned, it was a full day with the Bahls. Throughout the rest of the morning and into late afternoon, they relaxed around the pool. Shalini's mint couscous salad, served chilled with homegrown tomatoes, elicited the same accolades heard earlier on the court. The adults sipped Feni, an alcohol made from the cashew apple, perfectly suited to Jamnagar's humidity. Alessio had, almost unwillingly, begun to like his hosts.

Most of the discussion centered on the better points of

the morning's match, embellished as though four Federers had been on the court. When either Guhan or Vijay spoke of their own highlights, they were swiftly shot down by Alessio and Romil, who took turns reiterating the final score.

Once back in his hotel room, Alessio thought of the authentic joy the Bahls inspired in each other. They were a truly loving family, and he was a little startled to realize that he was growing envious of them. He wondered if he would ever have the chance to share in a similar love with a family of his own. He had had one of his best days of his life sharing time with this family he had just met, and something about this realization unnerved him. The day had revealed things about himself that he had never previously known or felt.

He decided to call Aprajita as planned, and found himself wondering if he actually missed her. Though usually ready to move on to business and the other points of conquest that mapped his days and life, he actually wanted this oddly joyful day to continue. He was determined to focus on the joy that Aprajita would provide him over the next couple of weeks.

"Aprajita, I won!"

"I knew you would! You have many skills."

"How about dinner this evening? You pick."

"I was thinking room service!"

"Wouldn't you prefer a proper dining establishment?"

"Why not make it easy? Let's do the same thing we did last night. I'm still in the mood for Italian food."

"I see a sea urchin in my future. How I enjoy splitting through the spines that seek to pierce, disarming their well-conceived defense, and for what? The tiny tender treasure inside that is succulent!"

"Ahhh, Alessio! Give me thirty minutes. See you then!"

"Meet at the bar downstairs. I need a drink!"

Aprajita didn't pack a suitcase, but she should have. The bed in her apartment would go unused for the duration of Alessio's stay.

As the production of the ceramic disks neared completion, Romil called Alessio to the facility one last time to summarize the design of the disks. He lectured in fine detail on the dismantled craft, which was more complicated than Alessio had realized from his cursory review of the blueprints.

"The upper ceramic disk, made watertight using the latest in high-pressure gasket technology, houses the control center. Everything is accomplished here, and it's programmable," Romil explained, noting the USB port. "But it's currently programmed per the instructions on the blueprints that any changes must be made by someone in this facility. This titanium tank holds the compressed air that inflates the Kevlar floats, making it virtually indestructible."

He then pointed to the port on the titanium air storage tank. "It's imperative that this is filled to exactly 100 PSI for every new launch. This is the GPS antenna, and this pod sends out a low-frequency ping, again as specified."

Romil pointed to the larger storage disk. "You'll note that this has a thicker layer of ceramic material, nearly four millimeters. The interior is built to house precisely 226.42 pounds."

He lifted the false bottom to the larger disk. "Here you have the motor for the jets. The intake valve is here, and these are the four jets that will make the necessary adjustments should any underwater currents attempt to capture the vessel. A laser gyroscope compass sends the data to the computer, which signals the jets to fire independently as required. It should come up within 100 meters of where it was dropped every time.

"The battery here needs to be replaced after each launch. Anyone can do it—it's a standard marine battery. The anchor bolts here will obviously also have to be replaced each time, again no problem. They're standard threaded bolts that we'll include with the delivery but you can purchase them anywhere."

He then drew his attention to the lead anchor. "This weighs 500 kilos as called for in the design. The small explosive cartridges mount here and are tied to the central computer using these special water environment connections. The anchor will be lost to the sea each time, of course. We have been commissioned to build twelve annually indefinitely. It's my understanding that we'll deliver two of the disks and twelve anchoring systems and store the other inventory here."

"Yes, that's right."

"Very good. We have designated a secure storage room in Plant Three for that purpose. I have included this manual but I must emphasize that except for the battery, filling the air tank, and the anchor systems, don't touch anything. The computer will provide real-time data after each recovery if there are any issues with any of the equipment. This CD can be loaded onto any laptop for this reporting. It's critical that these instructions are followed and the data be sent to our technicians each time."

Very impressive work, Alessio thought. His sources were to be commended, as were the efforts of those at Havikiran, particularly Romil, who he had grown to like tremendously. The pair had played three more matches with Romil's sons— all ending in the same outcome—over the course of the last two weeks.

Alessio believed that he had learned more on this assignment than on any other. He had even confided to Romil that his relationship with his family was strained, and Romil had provided advice that Alessio intended to implement. He expected to stay in touch with Romil, who he now considered a friend, and even invited his family to vacation in Rome during the Italian Open as his guest. Romil, however, didn't feel the same. For him, Alessio represented his organization and nothing more.

And there was Aprajita. Although their playing court was mostly his bed, they did rally at the tennis club one afternoon, though she lasted less than hour in the humidity and searing sun. In spite of this, he was impressed by her game.

Although she was the one who issued the challenge to play tennis, she didn't mention that she had played for the University of Florida women's varsity team on a tennis scholarship, an opportunity that allowed her to escape the severe poverty of her childhood. She had grown up on dirt floors, with no electricity and no running water.

With the delivery of the storage disks to a large cargo ship that came in to the Jamnagar port, the project was complete. The ship delivered several thousand liters of crude oil and left port with a couple of high-priced, fancy disks and ten complete anchoring systems. Throughout the exchange there was never any mention between Romil and Alessio that these disks were obviously designed with smuggling in mind.

As much as he bragged about his enchanting home in Rome, Alessio hadn't offered Aprajita any contact information and she hadn't asked. Neither one was quite sure whether a strong bond had formed. For two such independent people it usually took some time away to make that sort of determination. For now, they basked in their recently formed memories without an iota of regret.

There were no consequences when one embraced physical pleasures unencumbered by societal guilt. Indeed, the acceptance of truth, not externally imposed convictions, is vital to an existence free from shame.

Chapter 5: Fate Is Against Me in Health

Slipping back to the present, it seemed as though the entire village of Praiano was outside the entrance to the hospital in Naples, where Ciro had been transferred the previous night by helicopter. They waited, praying for good news.

Ciro had survived his open-heart surgery. The surgeon used venous graphs harvested from Ciro's leg and rerouted four clogged arteries to his heart. In medical parlance, he had undergone a coronary artery bypass grafting—hospital personnel referred to it as CABG, pronounced "cabbage." His condition remained critical as his brain has been deprived of oxygen for too long—he had suffered an anoxic brain injury, in hospital jargon.

Ciro's surgeon reported to the family that the likelihood of a positive outcome was doubtful. The surgeon advised that they would know more if—and here he particularly stressed *if*—Ciro made it through the next couple days. But he advised them to prepare themselves for the worst. Although open-heart surgery was one of the most stressful procedures the body could endure, the anoxic brain injury was in fact more distressing. He suggested that if Ciro did pull through, this would be the challenge for him to overcome. Then he allowed Ciro's parents and sister into his room. Amalia came with them, welcomed as a natural part of the nuclear family.

Ciro appeared lifeless. Tubes seemingly penetrated every part of his body. He was bloated, almost unrecognizable. A nurse stood by, monitoring what resembled a jet's cockpit of gauges and instruments. They each took turns standing over him, tears streaming, touching whatever part of his body they could reach, through sobs telling him how much he was loved.

They were allowed to stay in the room ten minutes before the nurse explained that they could visit for just ten minutes on three-hour cycles, as the next three days would be the most critical for his body to heal.

The mass of Praiano villagers gathered outside the hospital had enjoyed no emotional relief when Father Viglianti arrived. He had been parish priest of St. Gennaro for seven years. He had replaced Father Pesci, who had died tragically, apparently falling some four hundred feet from the coastal highway into a rocky ravine that adjoined the sea. It had taken several days to locate the missing priest, and many residents still found the event darkly intriguing.

In spite of Viglianti's refined masculine look and highly articulate style, he lacked charisma. His homilies, gospels, and interactions with the parish lacked the divinely inspired glow that had emanated from Father Pesci. In contrast, Viglianti's more contrived Mass rarely inspired anything that moved one's spirit to rejoice. In fact, many of the residents had switched to churches in either Positano or Amalfi to receive their blessings and fulfill their Catholic obligations.

The onlookers speculated that Viglianti had traveled to the hospital to perform the Sacrament of Last Rites. Although they were correct in this assumption, they underestimated the strength of his personal connection to Ciro and his family. Viglianti was stunned and hurt by Ciro's sudden calamity, and this was reflected in his panicked facial expression. In spite of his obvious grief, he greeted nearly everyone as he passed through the crowd.

He wished Ciro could witness the outpouring of love he saw before this hospital. The fresh realization that Ciro could not brought hot tears streaming down his face as he navigated the stairwell to Ciro's room.

Ciro's parents and sister huddled with Amalia, Francesca, their mother, Ote, and Juliana outside the room. They stood mostly in silent prayer, some tearfully holding one another.

They all looked terrified, an increasingly gaunt look that conveyed trauma and fear drawn out over hours of waiting. Each time one attempted to offer encouraging thoughts of hope, he or she broke down into uncontrollable sobs.

Father Viglianti went to Ciro's parents first. "My dear friend Lucio, how sorry I am for this pain. May God console you and provide you with the strength to lift you and your family through this tragic time."

Viglianti was about to continue when Lucio completely broke down, his frantic eyes pleading for a miracle. His wife and daughter clutched him tighter, all nearly hysterical. Viglianti spread his arms wide and hugged them for several long minutes.

Amalia was especially distraught. Her mother did her best to be the strength her daughter so desperately needed and Francesca held her tightly, but nothing ebbed her agony. Over and again she replayed the entire scene on the beach, hoping to wake from this terrible nightmare and convince herself that none of it was real.

After the priest arrived, Amalia sought refuge in the hospital's chapel. Her mother and sister helped carry her there. Her distraught appearance was wrenching for everyone they passed—the pain that plagued her was palpable.

Ote had vowed to Juliana that he would stay at the hospital until Ciro awakened. When one saw Ciro, they saw Ote. He somehow felt acutely responsible for the pain in all those surrounding him. His wife held him more tightly as he sobbed.

Once the surgery was complete, Ote had let himself believe that Ciro had rounded the corner to good health. He let himself dream that their lifelong routine would return. But the surgeon's latest update, coupled with the arrival of Father Viglianti, tore any vestige of protection from Ote's soul. The discovery that had briefly provided unimaginable joy for the two friends was now lost in the midst of his racing, desperate thoughts.

Four days after his surgery, Ciro was transferred from the CV ICU to the general ICU. Ote moved with him, still dressed in his evening attire, carefully planned for the Music on the Rocks that they never reached. His hair was now a tangled, greasy mess and his face sported the rough beginnings of a full beard. Even Amalia and Ciro's family had left on a few occasions to clean up and feebly try to emotionally restore themselves, but Ote kept his vow. No one could deter him from it, even when they complained about his increasing body odor.

The news brought by the physicians was never promising and rarely varied. Ciro remained in a coma. Only recently were they able to monitor his brain activity. These results showed the faintest glimmer of hope, but nothing definite.

Ote had gradually sunken into what seemed irreparable despair, believing he would never speak with his friend again. Suddenly, it occurred to him—the disk!

They had left the disk, though uncovered, at least concealed within the cave. This revelation, once it had flashed through Ote's mind, tormented him incessantly. Should he go secure the disk? He knew that Ciro, if he were able, would demand this of him. If Ciro were to wake, he would be mortified that Ote had abandoned the grandest of all prizes! It would likely put an end to his recovery.

The following day, having debated time and again, he said to Amalia that Ciro might improve if he weren't stinking up the hospital any longer. Over the past week, the two had shared many pensive hours together. She had noticed that as of late he was preoccupied and encouraged him to spend some time with his family. She urged him to show his family as much love as possible. "It's important to live every day as if it were your last," she said, "for you just don't know ..."

She hugged Ote again and again. She appreciated his faithfulness; she always had.

Chapter 6: Hateful Life

Ciro awoke nine days after his open-heart surgery. He was severely confused, and the sounds he heard were foggy and blurred. He could only hear and smell, while his other senses were virtually nonfunctional. Over several hours both his hearing and sense of smell would improve. These changes only further confused him, as did the conversations of those around him. His cognitive skills were improving at the same rate. This too confused him. He returned to sleep, confused and restlessly dreaming.

In his dream, he was playing soccer for the local club, clad in their bright bougainvillea-colored uniforms. It was a color he had not chosen; in fact he had put up quite a fight against it.

This home match was against Maori, just down the road from Praiano. He was thirteen, and there was talk that a representative from Napoli would be observing. He played the match of his life, scoring three goals from play and a fourth on a penalty kick as his team won 4–1. After the match, he and Ote were hiking home, up the winding, narrow roads, through shortcuts only accessible to pedestrians. They were young and they were happy. Here they could walk with arms around one another without suspicious glares. They were eating plums at Ote's house when the dream faded.

The next morning Ciro again awoke again and could now hear and smell more clearly. The voices were unfamiliar, the beeping noise constant, the smell a gross, bleached stench. He was thinking clearly, but his eyes refused to open. He also realized that his skin could not feel anything.

Mental orders to his hands, legs, and mouth all went ignored. He was baffled by these failed attempts. It was like someone admiring a M. C. Escher print, not from his Italian period but rather in the style of *Ascending and Descending*, appropriate for the Amalfi coast.

He recognized her smell as she entered the room—she always wore Dior. The smell gradually intensified. She bent down to kiss his cheek, her routine every day of the last week once they had removed most of his tubes.

"You're looking better today, Ciro!"

He could not feel her lightly massaging his hand.

"Do you know how much I love you?"

He did but he was unable to respond. What had happened? Where was he? He vainly tried to remember. He was fishing with Ote, hauling in the grouper—they thought they'd struck it rich, thought they'd caught a yellowfin. But then what happened?

He was listening keenly to Amalia, hoping for clues, when the neurologist entered.

"What happened to his friend?" the doctor asked.

"We finally convinced him to go home, clean up, and tend to his family."

"His vital signs have stabilized, which is promising, but the last test on his brain activity showed no improvement. Has the family considered the idea of organ donation?"

"He'll get better—give him time you, ass!"

"Well, you really don't have much say in it, do you?" the doctor remarked on his way out the door.

In the States, neither doctors nor nurses could broach the subject of organ donation, but they could be callous in their own way. Sometimes doctors appear harsh because the truth can be harsh.

It took Ciro several minutes to realize that they had been referring to him. In his mind, he was screaming to be heard, but he was the only one who could hear his own pleas. He heard Amalia crying uncontrollably, but he could not feel her tears as they landed on his arms as she tightly held his hand.

"Please dear God, please Ciro, you can't leave me … I cannot survive without you!"

In his mind Ciro joined her—he imagined his own tears. He had never faced a fear like this, not even when he was swept up by the fifteen-meter waves that once crashed into his property at One Fire. In an instant he, along with his tables, bar, kitchen equipment, umbrellas, and sun loungers, had been thrown into a blender set on puree.

That time he hadn't thought he'd make it out. The sea rarely spit one out alive when it was that fierce. Yet somehow he came through unscathed. That was two years ago. A puny prickle of fear compared to what he faced now. Mercifully, he lost consciousness again.

But this time nightmares intruded. An impossible task had been placed upon him. He stood on a vast expanse of a white sandy beach, miles long and hundreds of feet wide, an unfamiliar beach, and his task was to find the one grain of sand, one out of trillions, the one that would set him free. Again he awoke and it seemed to him that he was trembling.

Fortunately Ciro drifted into a more pleasurable sleep. He dreamed of the first time he and Amalia made love. Before Amalia, this would have taken place on the first or second date. But Amalia—oh, Amalia—was different.

He found joy in her eyes, her touch, her scent, and especially her laughter. In fact, she was the one who seduced him after seven months of dating. The thought hadn't even been on his mind. Sex was secondary. Sex could wait.

They had found themselves alone in Ciro's small apartment. They planned to hike to Nocelle, lunch at Donna Rosa, and hike back. The weather, however, didn't cooperate. It was a rainy, coldish winter day. They thumbed through the television stations a few times before Ciro asked if she wanted to bake a chocolate cake. He had the ingredients, and he had been planning to bake it for her the next day as a surprise.

When the cake was still batter, being stirred and added to, their playing started. She first doused his nose with a dab of the batter. Then she quickly moved to clean it up, using her tongue instead of the towel.

Ciro, never one to be outdone, slathered batter on her exposed neck. He took his time as thoroughly kissed her clean. She scolded him, warning him to be careful of her blouse for she didn't want it stained. She unbuttoned the blouse, as effortlessly as though she had been practicing the task in front of the mirror that morning. If she had practiced, her removal in front of Ciro was a consummate performance, enacted slowly with deliberate, drawn-out snaps of her fingers.

She wasn't wearing a bra, and he had seen her breasts a hundred times on the beach, where anyone could see her topless. He accommodated her shirtlessness with a double splatter of batter, one for each nipple. He teased the batter, softly flicking his tongue from one nipple to the other.

They kissed, their tongues exploring one another, and for the first time she touched him and measured the extent of his excitement. With his fingertips moving as lightly as feathers, he caressed her waist, just above her jeans, both hands moving in unison toward her navel then retreating.

She led him into his bedroom. Still standing, they slowly undressed each other. Once naked, they sank down to the bed and cradled each other, exploring their bodies with tender touches and tongues, but neither daring to proceed to lovemaking.

As they prolonged the play, their yearning mounted. After thirty minutes of intensely hot foreplay, Ciro looked deep into her eyes.

"I love you, my precious Amalia, with all my heart, and will always love you!"

"No one has ever touched me like this—not physically, but like my soul desires. I need you—I've loved you since we met."

With that she turned him onto his back. She hovered over him, touching his face, delicately gliding her mound upon him, undulating, increasing her motion, but mostly she tantalized, suspended above him. They locked eyes one last time; this confirmed what words never expressed. Slowly they joined, each focused on the other. Their escalating passion had finally won out.

Chapter 7: At This Hour without Delay

Gerardo had finally made it home for the first time in days. Juliana and their son, Gennaro, both lavished him with hugs and kisses.

"Ote, I'm so happy to see you, but please remove those clothes!"

"You stink, Papa!"

"Me? Stink?" Ote lifted Gennaro up and nuzzled him with his scraggly beard. "Papa doesn't stink, Papa doesn't stink, Papa doesn't stink!"

"Gennaro, come to Mama! Papa must clean up, he needs a shower before we go to dinner!"

Even Ote knew his clothes were beyond salvaging. The white linen pants he had slipped on eight days ago appeared to have fungus growing on them and were smeared with various unrecognizable stains. All the clothes that he had just peeled off were immediately thrown into the trash bin outside their small apartment.

"Why does Papa cry?" Gennaro asked his mother.

Juliana gathered her son into her arms. "Well son, it's Ciro, that's why Papa's been gone. He has been staying with Ciro who got sick and has to be in the hospital. Ciro is very sick and this makes us sad. We all love Ciro and it makes us sad that he isn't doing well, do you understand?"

"Is Ciro going to die like Grandpapa?"

"We hope not. We are going to go to the church and pray for him when Papa gets out of the shower. Then we will go down to Praia to eat? Does that sound good?"

"Will God save Ciro?"

With that Gennaro began to cry, not a tantrum like most six-year-olds. He maintained his composure even as tears still welled in his eyes. Juliana whisked him up above her head.

"I hope God answers our prayers, but only God knows what's best. Maybe it's better that Ciro join Grandpapa in heaven. Maybe Grandpapa misses Ciro!"

"I miss Ciro, Mama. I don't want him to go to heaven! He plays soccer with me and chases me. He and Papa, they promise to teach me fishing. They promise!"

"Papa will teach you but we all want Papa *and* Ciro to teach you, so we'll go to church and pray for him, okay? Now you go change into the shirt Mama put on your bed and wash that face of yours."

After Gerardo's shower, the Purpos walked hand-in-hand to St. Gennaro to pray. Lately the basilica had been quite busy, mostly filled with people offering prayers for Ciro.

Situated in Vettica Maggiore near La Statale and visible from the sea, St. Gennaro was often photographed by tourists. Residents and tourists alike gathered in its piazza. Built on an ancient foundation, the basilica's many cupolas had been recently restored with tiles in sparkling blue, gold, and white, which had been cut from locally quarried marble. They were the perfect contrast to the otherwise pale yellow stucco walls that rose some thirty feet into the air. Like most Catholic churches, it was a dominating edifice.

Centered atop the main cupola were six roman columns that formed the belfry. Its lofty octagonal coping was finished with smaller majolica tiles. As if guarding the impressive basilica, a taller, narrower tower cupola reached to the heavens. The tower housed a large round clock visible to those gathering in the piazza.

You entered the ornate basilica through double doors, five meters tall and made from ancient wood with an ever-darkening patina. The towering double entrance opened into a small narthex, the place for penitence.

The Romanesque nave, approximately forty feet long, was bright with cream marble floors. The marble was overlaid by a massive compass-like starburst in azure blue and yellow that ran the length of the central approach to the main altar.

Two rows of twenty mahogany pews framed the altar. Flanking each row were five arched alcoves that housed ancient treasures. Intricate plaster moldings throughout the basilica drew attention to these alcoves.

Vaulted some thirty feet high, the chancel was a semicircular dome, segmented by the same pale yellows, golden yellows, and seafoam green hues that dominated the basilica's interior paint scheme. Marble columns reaching to the dome framed the large tapestry of purple and gold depicting Praiano's patron saint, Gennaro.

Two ambries to each side of the columns were expertly sculpted marble, depicting simple biblical scenes. Equally ornate vestries surrounding the nave housed the basilica's sacred vessels and vestments.

A massive chandelier and two smaller flanking chandeliers hung above the main altar, illuminated by hundreds of yellow and orange bulbs that flickered as though they were flames. The altar was the center of all detail and design within the church; every aspect was intended to direct the penitent's soul and mind toward that central point.

Inside the basilica, Gennaro and Ote formed bookends around Juliana as the family knelt together facing *The Assumptions of 1696* by Giovan Bernardo Lama.

Please help Ciro get better, Gennaro prayed. *I miss him! I miss my Papa too, please help Papa and Ciro get better and tell Papa Alfonso I love him!*

Oh heavenly Father, place your loving, healing hands upon Ciro and all those who are suffering along with him, Juliana prayed. *Surround us with your generous uplifting spirit so that all might heal. Oh God, I fear most for Ote—I'm not sure he will survive without Ciro! Please, oh God, please hear my prayers. Ciro has so much yet to give—so many are so distraught, there are so many lives that ache. I fear that you alone, good Lord, can end this misery for us all. I pray that you will bestow through your loving touch, a healing miracle that will heal so many. Please God, I pray you will hear my prayers in Jesus' name.*

Ote's prayers were twisted in their desperation: *Lord, please, for I am to blame, do not punish Ciro for my thoughtless acts. You must see how Amalia is so terribly upset. I am to blame for this too. Please forgive me, dear Lord. Allow them to live their lives, to have the joy of children, and to see all the beauty that surrounds them that you have so provided. I pray that you will hold me accountable—only me! I don't know if you punish us for our discovery but I will gladly return this to the rightful owner—gladly, should your miraculous hand touch upon us! In this I pray.*

Ciro's parents stood in front of the altar. Surrounding them were Ciro's aunts and uncles, his cousins, their friends, and Father Viglianti. Every night this large contingent sorrowfully congregated in prayer, and Viglianti had grown to be an increasingly comforting presence to them all. The Pane family had warmly welcomed him, inviting him for dinner every Sunday since he arrived in Praiano. This was the way of the Amalfi coast.

Neither Viglianti nor Ciro could be blamed for their love of Sunday dinner at the Pane household. The matriarch Maria's simple menu, always composed of just-harvested ingredients, was:

Minestra di bietole, zucchine ed erbe fresche primavera con uovo molle e scampo scottato—a delicious light soup, especially when paired with *Fiano di Avellino Vadiaperti*, a nutty white wine with hints of pineapple.

Next, a *Spaghetti don Alfonso con pomodorini del piennolo* served with a simple regional red. On grand occasions they splurged for a bottle of *Timorasso Diletto Pomodolce*.

The last course before dessert was usually a *Pesce San Pietro cotto a bassa temperatura in extravergine di olive e clorofilla di limone con agretti*. A woody *Latour a Civitella Mottura* was a great compliment to this savory fish dish.

Dessert was what "kept 'em comin'"—Maria's *cioccolato*

cremoso, al latte e fondente, pinoli e gelato al croccante was legendary in Praiano, and always paired with a Pomele Falesco. It was a scrumptious meal.

Viglianti had enjoyed Ciro's company, usually talking trash about Ciro's Napoli side while extolling his beloved Roma. When the two teams met, they often watched the games at the local Bar del Sole. Viglianti enjoyed being the only Roma backer—his voice cheering when Roma scored a goal. There was pandemonium when Napoli scored.

Whether it was Signora Pane's cooking or the soccer debates with Ciro, Father Viglianti had grown to truly love the Pane family. His tears upon leaving the hospital were genuine and intense. He believed his Anointing of the Sick would be the last time he would see his friend alive.

Now he saw Ote praying with his family in the opposite corner of the basilica. He excused himself from the Panes and touched Ote's shoulder, squeezing gently, wishing he could absolve Ote of his pain.

Though they were only in the basilica for ten minutes or so, the visit helped lift the Purpos' spirits. Holding his family close to him was what Ote most needed at that time. With their spiritual yearnings momentarily satisfied, Ote and his family were having a difficult time deciding how best to satiate their hunger pains.

Walking arm-in-arm along the main coastal highway, they were often forced to squeeze tightly against various storefronts as the traffic nudged by them. Locals, who stopped them every few steps to give their best wishes and ask for updates on Ciro's condition, were an even bigger hindrance. Finally they escaped down a narrow residential shortcut.

Seated at the Bar Mare Petit Restaurant, Juliana and Ote gave Salvatore Pisacane all the latest news about Ciro. Gennaro played on the beach with another child around his age. They were building a rock fort, which they would soon reduce to rubble with stone rockets.

"I just don't know, Salvatore. He might never make it. I can tell you this—he wouldn't want to live unless he could live as he did before. I can't even bear to go in and see him—I just sit outside the room praying."

"Have faith, Ote. Only God knows best! I can't imagine life without Ciro but God takes so many of the young. I sometimes wonder why, but this only torments me. How am I to know such things?"

"I often wonder—too often!"

"Ote, you have done all you can do, it's not in our hands any more," Juliana said with tears in her eyes. "We must trust in God's knowing hands now. I will be here for you no matter what. And your other friends—reach out to them, Ote. Your son there—keep him in your thoughts, Ote! We'll get through this!"

"Is there a better wife than mine, Salvatore?"

"She's one of the best—she has to be! And she's right, Ote. We are all here for you, so don't try to get through this time alone! I have to return to work but I understand you're going to take the Zodiac out tonight. Would you like some company, maybe share some classic Ciro stories?"

"That's a great idea. Not tonight—I wouldn't be very good company—but soon. Tonight I need to gather my thoughts."

Returning to La Praia was complicated for Ote. Just over a week before, he had been crashing the boat ashore. It was also the place of thousands of vivid memories made with Ciro. They had come to this restaurant thousands of times. Family-owned for decades, it was run by Mama Maria, the Sophia Lauren of La Praia. At 82, her cooking was unmatched.

"Gennaro, try the octopus," Juliana said. "It's delicious."

"It's yucky!"

"At least try it," Ote added. "It's good for you—it makes you strong!"

"It not help Ciro. He love awfulpuss."

"Excuse me a second buddy, Daddy has to—" But before Ote could finish, his tears consumed him. Abruptly he bolted up and staggered away.

Gennaro followed and found his papa hunched over, hiding in the shadows and bawling. Gennaro hugged his father's leg.

"I'm sorry, Papa. I not want make you cry!"

But Gerardo couldn't answer.

"Did Mama tell you I juggle ball now one minute? I practice when you gone."

Gerardo's tears persisted as he lifted his son with a big hug. He even managed a guttural noise of affirmation.

"You know why I practice? I want beat Ciro's record. I want show Ciro when he better!"

Gerardo hugged him tighter, but the latest images Gennaro provoked tore at him, and he gasped for air as his sobbing became more audible.

Everyone heard him, the tourists, Salvatore and his staff, and Juliana, who rushed over to his hiding spot. She'd never seen Gerardo this distraught, not even when his father had passed away a year earlier. By the time she reached them, Gennaro was crying too.

"Gennaro, you go back over and see if you can help Salvatore, okay? Papa just needs a little time."

"I want stay here. I want help Papa."

I am so fortunate, Ote thought but he was still unable to speak. So he hugged them both, the best he could do. After several minutes of hugs, his sobs gradually diminished.

Gerardo, feeling like everyone's eyes were upon him, led his family back to their table. He felt guilty for being such a miniscule man. When Salvatore came over and squeezed his shoulder, Ote gave him a soggy, tight smile and lowered his head.

"Papa look, I eat the awfulpuss, watch! I be strong like you."

Me, strong? he thought. *Hardly! Look at me.* "I think you are already stronger than your papa."

"I think you Supaman!"

"Oh, I'm Superman all right, G, but I'm stuck in a mine full of kryptonite and can't escape."

"Ote!" Juliana exclaimed.

"What skiptinite?"

"Don't listen to your papa, Gennaro. Sometimes he's silly!"

"It's kryptonite—crip ton night—but Mama's right, I was just being silly. How 'bout you try another piece of octopus, then maybe we can have some gelato before I have to go and work a little bit."

"I want cocolot!"

"It's chocolate!" Juliana corrected.

After more "awfulpuss" and some delicious "cocolot" gelato, Gerardo bid them good-bye. He excused himself on the pretext that he needed to spend some time checking on work. He had forgotten that Salvatore had already given up on him and that Juliana knew his real intent. At ten that evening, the sun finally having set, Ote headed out toward Positano aboard his boat.

He spent his first three hours drifting out to sea. Sifting through memories, he remembered the first time he and Ciro had smoked a joint. Ote had stolen one from his older brother. Earlier that year they had smoked their first cigarette, stolen from his father. Here, petty theft was best kept in the family.

"Look what I have!"

Ciro had grimaced. "Ugh, cigarettes make me want to hurl."

"It's not a cigarette. It's a reefer."

"Dope?"

"Yup, it will make us laugh!"

"It'll get us busted. Where'd you get that? Here, let me see it."

"I found it in Pietro's drawer. I tried to get him to smoke with me but he said I was too young. But I've smelled it and I've seen him and Luigi after they smoked some. They just kept laughing!"

"Is that why you're wearing your soccer uniform? You're not going swimming?"

"Do you want me to drown? Hell no, I'm not swimming. It'll probably make us like when we were drunk."

Ciro made another face. "I'll never drink again. Just thinking about it makes me sick all over again."

"This won't make us sick, though. That's why they smoke it!"

"We'll get in trouble again, and this time they won't let us off so easy. They'll kill us!"

"They won't even know. It'll be our secret. It's not the same as beer. Pietro's always getting high and my parents never catch him."

"Well, it might be fun to try it at least once. Do you smoke it like a cigarette?"

"Yeah, but you hold your breath as long as you can so you don't waste it."

"How do *you* know?"

"I heard Pietro, that's how. He told Ludovica to hold it."

"Ludo smokes weed?"

"Hell, yeah. Everybody does."

"Isabella doesn't. My mom and dad would kill her!"

"Not if they didn't know. But you're right, I doubt Isabella smokes anything."

"It will make us hallucinate!"

"That's what so fun!"

Ten minutes later they were both laughing, still waiting to hallucinate. "Check this out, Purpo," Ciro yelled into the wishing well near the Africana's grotto, where they'd finally lit it up. "HI!" And the well echoed back *Hi, hi, hi.* They both screamed with laughter. "Purpo's nuts, but he's got no nuts!"

The well replied *Nuts, nuts, nuts …*

"Lick nuts, Pane!" *Pane, Pane …*

"Eat poop, Gerturd!" *Turd, turd …*

And by now they were rolling with laughter.

"What are you kids doing? Have you finally lost your minds?" demanded Luca, the owner of the Africana and Gerardo's uncle.

Both boys froze, paranoia replacing their euphoria in an instant. They looked at each other, now very much afraid.

Luca picked the roach off the rim of the well. "Well, that explains it. What do we have here, boys? Looks like marijuana. Smells like it too. Now if it were yours, Ote, I'd have to give it to your mother, wouldn't I? You wouldn't want me to keep a secret from my own sister, would you?"

"It's mine, Signore Milano! Ote didn't even try any of it. Please don't tell my parents! I promise I just tried a couple puffs, you know, just experimenting."

"You don't have to lie to me, Ciro. Just take it away. If I ever hear that you kids are smoking this crap again, I'll tell both of your parents. Now get out of here before I change my mind!"

Ciro quickly put the remains of the joint in the front pocket of his trunks and sped away with a thank you. Gerardo gave his uncle a kiss on the cheek and with a quick hug and a few thanks, then raced to catch up with Ciro.

"Great idea, Purpo!"

"He's not going to say anything."

"Let's go to the soccer field and practice. I need to work off some of these shakes."

"We don't have our ball."

"My house is on the way, idiot!"

"Girl!"

"Wuss!"

"Pansy!"

Their affectionate insults kept flying all the way to Ciro's house. A few minutes later, Ciro walked back out with the soccer ball.

"What took you so long? Oh, you had to change out of your swim trunks? Only a wuss would think they needed soccer shorts."

"Only a girl would think this hurts!" Ciro gave Ote a quick punch to his arm. They fell to the ground wrestling but were soon interrupted by Ciro's mother.

"Potheads!" Maria shrieked. "Get back here, you potheads!"

Oops, it seemed somebody forgot to remove the roach from their swim trunks. They were banned from playing soccer or hanging out with each other for the entire summer.

And as Ote's mind returned to the present, he was crying again. But it was finally late enough to embark on his current mission, so he pulled the boat's motor to a start and made his way back to the coastline.

At one in the morning, the Africana was as deserted as he had hoped. He worried about the disk; its hiding space was never meant to last this long. What if it had been discovered? He landed the zodiac and ran toward the entrance, cracking his head along the way on a rock jutting from the grotto walls.

To his relief, the gray disk was there, although completely exposed. The top was lying askew against a rock and could have been seen from the outside had anyone bothered to look inside.

He knew that it was too cumbersome and heavy for him to carry alone, but he hadn't even considered bringing in a third conspirator. He decided to remove the contents to lighten the load. It took him nearly thirty minutes to empty the disk and conceal its contents in nooks and crannies well above the waterline. No one area could have accommodated this mother of all loads, so he scattered it all across the grotto.

Not even handling the life-changing contents brought a smile to Ote's face. That he had been here with Ciro just eight days before was agonizing.

With the cargo offloaded, the disk was of a more manageable weight and with some effort he dragged it back to the rocky entrance and into his boat. He loaded the disk with rocks and reattached every third star screw or so. It wasn't important that it was waterproof; rocks like water.

His plan disintegrated when he took out his knife and stabbed at the float that formed the bottom perimeter. You can't pierce Kevlar with a bullet, let alone a knife.

After fifteen minutes of trying and failing to slash open the inflatable rafts, Ote removed star screws from the top and took out the rocks. Then he discovered the false bottom. He finally started to sense what he was dealing with. Its sophistication scared him.

Once the guts of the thing were exposed, he tackled the outside of a metal flow valve with his quickly dulling knife and screwdriver, prying, banging, and tearing until the disk began to spin with a great whoosh. Success—the floats deflated. He wasn't sure what all the wiring was for but decided better safe than sorry and cut through most of the wires, though he missed a few. He reloaded the rocks and fastened even fewer star screws this time, saving the rest to throw into the sea.

He went out about one mile from the coast, closer than he would have if destroying the floats hadn't taken so much time.

He scuttled the disk, releasing it to the seafloor, which was nearly five hundred meters deep at this point. Right after releasing the disk, he felt a shudder of panic and wondered if maybe he should have held on to the thing.

He missed Ciro. Moving the disk's contents to a more secure location, Ote concluded, was impossible for one person. He tried to persuade himself that he needed his friend's hands, not his wisdom, but deep down he knew that wasn't so. Ciro had always made the better decisions. He also realized suddenly that he hadn't counted the packages that he had hidden.

Ciro would have thought to count the packages, no doubt about it. This thought brought a renewed stream of tears to Ote's eyes. As he returned to La Praia, he passed the Saracen tower, shaped like the Washington Monument though built of more ancient, less-honed rock. He used to play with Ciro near the base of this tower in their younger days.

Meanwhile, farther out to sea, a ship heard the first of sixty pings emitting from the disk. Applause suddenly filled the control room. Then suddenly the transmission was lost. The captain ordered the navigator to plot the mark and steam immediately in that direction.

Chapter 8: As Fancy Takes It

Angela was stunned when Gio invited her aboard his yacht as a thank you for her efforts with Ciro. She had seen many large yachts cruising along the Amalfi coast and often dreamed of being invited aboard one. She and Todd were told to meet the yacht's tender in Positano.

They were welcomed aboard by Gio and his companion, an enticing Spanish woman half Gio's age. She was stunning—tall and slender with short, cropped black hair and perfect English. From the look of her skin it seemed she spent most of her time tanning. The diamonds in her ears sparkled in the early afternoon sun.

Gio, on the other hand, did not dress the part of the billionaire playboy that he was. His slacks were purchased off the rack, as they had always been. Usually he wore an oversized t-shirt, but on this day he was wearing an untucked, half-buttoned long-sleeved shirt.

But he was wearing cufflinks to match his gold wristwatch, the only jewelry he ever wore—indeed, he only accessorized on special occasions. And his caramel-blond hair was slicked back, which also subtly marked this as a special occasion. He had even taken time to shave. Although he was very meticulous and organized with a thoroughly detail-oriented mind, his friends knew him as Sloppy Gio.

He was a decent-looking man, around six-foot-three with a fit, athletic body. But it wasn't his looks that captivated. He was intent and engaged seriously with everyone. He focused on the way that words were said as much as to *what* was actually said. He always, quite instinctively, sought clues.

Gio wasn't at all arrogant or demeaning. He considered his fortune something that must be shared. Although he did maintain an entitled attitude that conveyed a pride of accomplishment, he never assessed others based on their means or position in life.

Most of his time was spent lavishing his family, especially his parents, with love. His two older sisters and his three older brothers all held high-ranking positions within his empire. They often gathered together on the yacht.

Gio didn't sit around counting his money or worrying about the daily fluctuations of his wealth. He had hired people to worry about those things for him. His CFO was an American who had been caught up in one of Wall Street's periodic scandals. Gio had hired him directly out of prison. They had been roommates back at Duke University and had maintained their friendship ever since. The CFO reported to Gio's oldest brother, Carlo, who ran the entire privately held organization.

All of Gio's friends were from his pre-wealthy past. He had never attempted to befriend a fellow plutocrat, always assuming that the only thing they had in common were just numbers, and numbers really didn't inspire Gio.

His yacht, the *Thetis*, measured nearly fifty meters in length and was made of brilliant white fiberglass. It was named for the queen of the Nereids, the sea nymphs of ancient Greek mythology who came to the aid of drowning sailors. She was said to be the mother of Achilles.

The exterior deck was thin-slatted teak, and the outside dining table was made of the same tropical hardwood. Situated on the upper deck of the three-story ship was a hot tub large enough to accommodate eight people.

During the brief tour of his yacht, Gio noted that they kept the tub cool during the hot summer months and rarely used it as a "hot" tub, more of a plunge pool to cool off. Angela and Todd were impressed with the main salon, a four-hundred-square-foot space complete with Mark Levinson stereo components. The room had two leather couches, each measuring nine feet in length, very contemporary in design and off-white in color. Most of the walls were paneled with light-stained wood, with darker shades complimenting the interior walls.

They were led to another salon devoted to television viewing, as well as an office, a fitness room, and dining room. The entire yacht was masterfully designed and outfitted with only the best in furnishings. The tour didn't include the crew's quarters, bedrooms, galley, or the control room where the captain helmed the luxurious yacht.

Todd and Angela were especially inquisitive about the three jet skis that were stored on the lower deck. Apparently Gio noted this interest and whispered something to one of the crewmembers, who more closely resembled security guards than wait staff.

They lunched on fresh lobster that Gio had flown in from Maine, along with Krug cuvée. Angela had to ask for melted butter, which Gio understood as an American eccentricity.

"Would you like to take out the jet skis?" Gio asked them after lunch.

"We don't have our swimsuits," Angela responded a bit wistfully.

"Yes, you do, Dr. Neurmer!"

The staff member returned with a pair of La Perla swimsuits. He ushered them to the guest suite that was larger, and even more immaculate, than a suite at the Four Seasons. After changing, Todd and Angela spent the next hour jet-skiing and laughing.

After they returned to the yacht and changed back into their clothes, Gio broached the idea of Angela taking over Ciro's case. Normally she would have never considered such a proposition, but Ciro was a friend. In response she pointed out the obvious: she wasn't licensed to practice in Italy and had no medical malpractice insurance here. She had no privileges at the hospital and was unfamiliar with the local medical equipment. But perhaps she could consult unofficially?

Angela was surprised to learn that every obstacle she had

mentioned had already been resolved. Gio explained that Father Viglianti had convinced him to step in and help. Although Gio didn't know Ciro, he quickly agreed for the sake of all those in the area who had welcomed him with open arms.

"I know that I'm interrupting your vacation," Gio said, "and I realize that you recently retired. And I know there are no guarantees of a good outcome. But if anyone can help, I know you can! You have already saved his life. I would consider it the highest favor for me. I can offer you a half million Euro to retain your services, plus ten thousand Euro per hour. Should your efforts prove successful, you can have your choice of any of my four villas here. I have already taken the liberty of arranging your stay at the San Pietro. My helicopter will shuttle you daily from there to Naples. With just one patient to tend to, you should be back home to join your husband by lunch. If you need anything, including your own staff, I can have them flown in on my personal jet. And if you need different medical equipment, I will make it happen. It's important that we do our best to save this young man, to give him back his life."

As Angela and Todd took the tender back to Positano, they could hardly contain their enthusiasm. In the excitement of the day, they were largely oblivious to how much information Gio had gathered about them. He served them their favorite lunch (albeit at first without melted butter) and favorite champagne, and he even knew that Angela had long dreamed of owning anything La Perla. Despite making a tidy living as a neurosurgeon, she was not one to spend five hundred dollars on a swimsuit.

Her assignment was set to begin the next day. That evening they checked into the San Pietro, one of the finest hotels in the world. That, coupled with the chance to earn a multimillion-dollar villa, had them up all night like two kids unable to sleep on Christmas Eve.

Chapter 9: Shadowed and Veiled

Alessio Bianco was heading to the Fiumicino airport with his racquets packed. For once his trip was all about pleasure—he hoped it wouldn't be interrupted by a call on line two, but it was impossible to predict when those would come.

When he signed on years earlier, the parameters of his employment were established. He could travel anywhere he wanted without any notification to anyone. But he had only left Europe three times over the years, as work came first, regardless of the circumstances.

One year into his new job, his father had passed away after a long, gutsy battle with colon cancer. And on the day before his father's funeral, line two rang. He had naively expected some compassion his employer. But of course, he was wrong, and never questioned the parameters of his job again. His mother and his only brother hadn't spoken to him since. He tried to explain that he had no choice, but his explanation lacked the necessary specifics. He could tell no one the truth. He didn't even know the truth.

He and his brother Vincenzo had been constant companions growing up. The played tennis like their friends played soccer—every day. They bickered over every close line call. These arguments prematurely ended match after match, but they always forgave one another. Within no time, they'd be back out crushing the ball. Clay was their favorite surface—they were sliders. They dreamed of playing at Wimbledon; it seemed incredible that anyone could play tennis on grass.

Alessio had sent Vincenzo an invitation to join him at Wimbledon this year, all expenses paid. By making amends with his brother, his brother could influence his mother. She had just turned seventy and was still in great health. He kept track of them by various means, desperately wanting to be a part of their lives. He had been denied an opportunity to be an uncle, a brother—and most of all, a son—for too long. But the invitation to his brother was returned unopened; Vincenzo had refused delivery. Rather than enraging Alessio, it spurred a torrent of tears. He knew the truth: he was unloved by everyone. So he was on his way to London alone.

His dampened spirits were low enough to exceed even the dreary, rainy conditions that greeted him upon touchdown at Gatwick on the second Sunday of Wimbledon. He had tickets to the Ladies and Gentlemen's semifinals and finals on Centre Court—for this, like so many other aspects of his odd, surreptitious life, he had sources. His brother's seat was now a lure to his conquest, though he didn't really need a lure. Adept manipulation of others had become a second nature.

Alessio was staying at the May Fair hotel adjoining Green Park, centrally located in London. Surrounded by pubs and restaurants and an easy walk to Soho, Piccadilly, Hyde Park, the West End Theater District, and the Buckingham Palace, it was an upscale hotel catering mostly to business types. For attractions not in the immediate vicinity, a Tube stop was only a block away.

His itinerary for his first few days would largely be occupied by a tour of the city. It was his first time in London, as business had never brought him here, though he had often dreamed of a perfectly timed (in other words, during the Wimbledon weeks) business-related excuse to come. He spoke the English language fluently and was wise enough to pack an umbrella.

After checking into the hotel, he immediately headed out to scout the area. He never sought the recommendations of the concierge, instead relying on his sources. They knew his particular drug of choice: the conquest. To him, it was all about the thrill of the chase. Only once in his life had he enjoyed the actual sex more than the pursuit, and that was some two years ago in India.

He was on his way to Club 366, near Hyde Park, to begin his evening with a cocktail. He could use a drink, but even more, a new conquest.

After ordering a gin and tonic from the bar, it didn't take him long to spy a prospect. He took a seat at a table next to two attractive women in their late twenties. He noticed one stealing glances at him, his first smile in London. Soon they invited him to their table. When he saw how they reacted to his Italian accent, he thought perhaps he could have them both. It wouldn't have been the first time.

They laughed, inquired, and flirted over the next hour. The women were especially interested in discussing Rome, one of their favorite cities.

"I love the Trevi Fountain area but always stay near the Spanish Steps, at the Van Gogh Hotel. Are you familiar with it?"

"Ah, there are so many wonderful hotels, large and small, though I must say that I have no knowledge of that one. But I do like the works of Van Gogh. I was just at an exhibit at the Citta Moderna. His works were brought in from everywhere—the Louvre, New York, everywhere. Mostly his early works that were influenced by his Christian upbringing, as his father was a minister. His paintings lacked color then, before his French influences."

"You're not only gorgeous, but smart too!" the brunette said, twirling her hair with a smile.

Her blonde companion was even bolder. "I'd like to see your hotel, Alessio!" As she spoke, her fingertip gently caressed the side of the brunette's neck, behind her ear.

The brunette smirked. "Would like to join us for dinner at the Veeraswamy?"

"I would be delighted to join you, wherever you'd like to go."

"Let's do room service back at your hotel, Alessio," the blonde offered.

"Ashley, that's a bit forward, don't you think!"

"Is it more or less forward than this?" Ashley slid her hand between the buttons of her friend's blouse and started to massage the brunette's nipple.

"Do you like that, Avril? Does it make you hot? How about you, Alessio? Care to join in?"

Alessio smiled. "You two certainly have captivated my attention. Let's have dinner at the Ver-place you mentioned, Avril, then take Ashley up on her fantastic idea to have dessert in my room. How's that for a wonderful compromise?"

Ashley smiled and gave her friend's breast a final squeeze. "Okay! Let's eat a quick dinner and take our time with the dessert course. Allow me to pick up the bar tab … since you're providing the dessert and all."

After she paid the bill, the threesome strode arm-in-arm-in-arm and hurried through the rain. The girls, now even more animated, soothed his aching heart. He almost felt loved.

The 1920s-era restaurant, resplendently decorated in shades of purple and orange, served a delicious Kashmiri *rogan josh*, a lamb curry seasoned with saffron and cockscomb flower.

"Ladies, dinner was delicious, much like your company."

"So are you ready for desert, Alessio?" Ashley asked as she slyly slid her hand under the table to grope his inner thigh.

"But I thought we decided to go to that club Avril mentioned to get warmed up. You should see my dancing—it'll likely make you laugh!"

"I'm warmed up already!"

"Me too," said Avril. "And I'm hungry for something sweet and tasty!"

Tramps, Alessio thought with a smile. *But maybe there's fun in being the pursued for a change. So which one shall earn the right to sit beside me at Wimbledon?*

Alessio gestured for the waiter. "Sir, we're finished here, and we have a pressing matter to attend. Is my bill prepared?"

As Alessio waited for the check, he spotted an attractive Indian girl through the window. Surely his eyes were playing tricks; his subconscious trying to convince him she was real. But he knew himself well enough to know that his eyes didn't play tricks. He excused himself, promising to return shortly, explaining that he thought he had seen an old friend unexpectedly pass by.

Meanwhile, at around the same time back in Praiano, a midnight-blue Bugatti Veyron pulled in front of Pane villa. There wasn't really a parking spot, so Gio left just enough room on the roadway for other vehicles to pass.

As he rapped on Pane's front door, he focused on his mission. *She must be pure, not broken. I need her, but as she was, not how she is. I can't influence a shredded soul ... I speak to that very truth. Just stay focused.*

"Hello, may I help you?" Lucio Pane asked.

"Oh, excuse me, I must have been lost in thought. Signore Pane?"

"Yes."

"My name is Dr. Giocondo Benvenuto. My friend, Francisco Vigilante—uh, Father Vigilante—told me the very sad news regarding your son. May I come in?"

"But of course, Dr. Benvenuto, a pleasure to meet you," Lucio said as he shook Gio's hand and welcomed him into his home.

"Please have a seat. Mariaaaa! We have a guest! MARIA!"

"I heard you, dear. I was organizing some of Ciro's pictures. Oh my, I know you! Well, I don't really *know* you ... You're Gio, yes?"

"Dear, it's Dr. Benvenuto."

"It's Gio, Signore and Signora Pane!" he said, rising to greet Maria. "As I was just saying to your husband, Father Viglianti has told me about the tragic news regarding your son. Please, let's all have a seat."

Lucio and Maria shared a perplexed expression as they all sat down.

"What a great pleasure to meet you, Gio," Maria managed.

"Please—it is my pleasure to meet my neighbors. I just wish it were under more favorable circumstances. And if I may, please beg my pardon for my interloping, but I am here to help."

"I don't understand, Dr. Benvenuto. I understand your position and all … but I'm not sure you *can* help?"

"All we can do is to try, Signore. And please, really, let's drop any formality. Please call me Gio. In fact, why not call me Sloppy Gio? I fear given my inexperience that I may, perhaps, come across as sloppy and apologize in advance. But as I said, all anyone can do is to try."

"Yes, without question, Gio. And dropping any pretense, I am Lucio. Many know me here as Lunatic Lucio. And my wife, Maria, most believe she's mad as well, but only for marrying me!"

They all laughed. The ice was broken.

"You're very clever, Lucio. As for my offer, please don't allow your pride to interfere. I know that you're both quite humble, like everyone on the coast. This is for Ciro."

"But I still don't understand, Gio. Money can't cure our son, not even your money. And I hope you'll excuse me for saying so."

"You're an attorney, Lucio, are you not?"

"Yes, but—"

"Then you understand more than most the complexity of gray areas, where truth and belief collide. I will only profess the truth and will not delve into hope. Hear the truth, for time is short."

Lucio and Maria shared another perplexed look as Gio continued.

"Please keep in mind that I have already made arrangements for Ciro to receive the best care possible. I merely need your approval. Did you get a chance to meet Dr. Angela Neurmer, the tourist from New York who helped to save your son?

"We haven't yet but hope to," Maria said. "Ciro's friend Ote told us about her. They're both heroes to us!"

"She happens to be the best neurosurgeon in the world.

She's known Ciro for years, many years, and she's agreed to take over his care. I've hired her, if you'll allow me?"

"You hired her?" Lucio asked. "I don't understand."

"Yes, and she's agreed, I think mainly because of the time she's spent with your son. She loves it here, so much so that she and her husband are moving here. She wants to help too."

Before they could answer, Gio continued. "It's at no cost to you, of course. I have been so fortunate to call this place home. Please allow me to return only a portion of my gratitude to our home."

"Why do you say she's the best?" Lucio asked.

"Because she *is* the best. I know this to be true. If she weren't, I'd bring in the best."

"Maria, how can we possibly turn down this very generous offer?"

"It's a miracle!"

"Take a cautious stance. She may be the best, but she offers no promises. She hasn't yet had a chance to review your son's charts and assess his condition. Even with her, there are no guarantees."

"Our prayers have been answered, Lucio!"

"But we must remember, she isn't God. Only God knows what's best, Maria, and we must continue to pray." Lucio reached out and shook Gio's hand. "Dr. Benvenuto—uh, Gio—from the bottom of our hearts, one thousand thanks!"

Gio smiled and stood up. "I've taken too much of your time already, and I might be parked illegally. If you'll excuse me, I'll let Dr. Neurmer know."

He gave them his cell number and insisted that if they needed anything, emphasizing *anything*, they should phone him without hesitation. And with that he set an envelope on the table in front of them.

"Please, take this—it will help reduce the financial burdens that arise in such a tragic time."

He didn't give them an opportunity to decline his offer,

instead turning for the door.

Lucio opened the envelope as soon as Gio left. It contained €50,000. Chump change for Gio, perhaps, but a year's salary for Lucio. Gio was not one to profligately toss his money around—his munificence was always lined with motive.

The Panes were utterly overwhelmed by the generosity of this man. Maria called Amalia, then Ote, then the others to share the good news. If it was Gio's intent to become an instant hero, he had succeeded.

At about the same time Alessio was enjoying the sights of London and Gio was giving the Panes hope, the Chief Executive Officer sat in his office and fumed. His office was immaculate, the size of a basketball court and decorated with ancient treasures. It had the latest in secure communications technology, and his messages were delivered around the world more securely than those of the president of the United States. Indeed, his office was more influential.

But his office was now also vulnerable. A simple failure like the losing of the disk—more important, the contents of the disk—could lead to a world in turmoil, to the collapse of the greatest businesses around the globe. There was a near miss when customs boarded their ship and almost found the shipment. They were looking for weapons of mass destruction but they would bask in any discovery.

Several years back, the world had changed. The fear that terrorists might smuggle biological or nuclear weapons meant increased security around the globe, especially with American allies. No longer could smugglers drop their contraband near the shore, mark it by global positioning satellite, and later have divers return to recover it. Their ships were targeted by customs near shore, and farther out to sea by the coastal guards. This increased security led to the conception of the disk. Following its invention and implementation, the disk had faithfully worked as designed on twenty-five previous drops. The fact that this disk had recently been serviced due to an error code that mandated the replacement of the GPS module led the CEO to believe that it was during this replacement when something had gone wrong.

Their sources along the coast confirmed that there was no news of anyone discovering the disk, and surmised that it was unlikely anyone could have discovered it without revealing its secret. They had brought in an unmanned submersible to search the seafloor without success. They concluded that the disk had never disengaged from its anchor, and the area was simply too vast to adequately sweep. They would address this failure with a second-generation disk that had redundancies of critical components. They planned to improve upon the signal, making it detectable even when several thousand feet below the surface.

"Where was the project managed?" the CEO demanded.

"Havikiran," answered one of the four members of his senior management team

The CEO had asked the wrong question. *Who designed the disk?* would have been better, and *Who screwed up this drop?* would have been the best. His was a lazy logical conclusion that discounted their own loading process post-servicing when one distracted technician whose job it was to establish the connection to the disk's onboard computer and verify that the programming wasn't corrupted—the last step before the disk was sealed. It was a step they took each time. With the accidental stroke of one key, their man advanced the date of the disk's release by one day.

It was also decided amid the opulence of this all too powerful office that any competent manufacturer should have challenged the design of the disk. These redundancies and added signal strength were important design flaws and the last line of defense had failed to recognize that fact. The final line of defense would never make a mistake like this again. The CEO would place a secure call to Alessio Blanco. The CEO had never met him, but he appreciated Alessio's perfect track record.

Chapter 10: Ever-Waning Fate

Upon her arrival at the hospital via Gio's helicopter, Angela was relieved to see that Ciro's chart had already been translated into English. Her first protocol was to examine the test results, the accompanying treatment plan, and Ciro's condition since it had been implemented. An anoxic brain injury could ultimately lead to a complete recovery or death, as well as every shade of variation in between the two extremes. After nearly two hours of scouring the data, she made her first visit to her new patient before reporting her findings to the family.

It was standing room only in and around Ciro's room. Everyone was enthused to see the famous Dr. Neurmer assuming the leadership of the case.

After clearing the room of everyone except Ciro's parents, Amalia, and Angela's translator, Angela proceeded with her evaluation.

"Keep in mind how difficult it is for me to tell you what I've concluded about the situation. The present information doesn't bode well for Ciro. I will verify this information and all of his vital signs, and I've ordered a new round of tests to make that determination. Prior to the tests we are going to remove his breathing tube and discern whether he is capable of breathing on his own. If he is not, I'd suggest that he be allowed to rest in peace for the remainder of his time, but of course it's ultimately up to you to make that determination. I am not questioning the current patient care plan, though I certainly would have done things differently. That doesn't mean I am definitely right, but an aggressive care plan from the onset does tend to yield better outcomes. After the tests, if we even get to this stage, I will adjust his plan of care accordingly. It's not really the time for questions now but if you have any

I'll do my best to answer them based on the data that I've already gathered."

"So we remove the tube," asked Lucio, "and he dies if he can't breathe without it?"

"I want to see if Ciro has a chance. I know this must pain you—the truth in crises like this is often very painful. I'll give your family time to discuss this. If you decide to change his status indicating you do not want to resuscitate, you'll need to meet with a social worker to sign the paperwork. If you wish to continue with the tube, I will understand, but will then need to vacate my role as his doctor."

There were no further questions, so she left them to contemplate.

Ciro had heard it all. He tried not to listen, desperately tried to escape this torture cell, in his mind his condition was truly harsher than death, one he couldn't escape without death's assistance.

He felt like the forlorn hero who ejects from a helicopter some fifteen hundred meters up, plummeting to the ground at more than three hundred kilometers an hour, his face fluttering violently upward, squinting to keep the wind from blowing his eyes out. In his desperate vision it seemed impossible that his dinner jacket wasn't ripped away by the F4 winds, and yet the jacket wasn't even smacking him on the face.

Screaming through the air, our desperate hero was wise enough to recall the napkin that he earlier stole from a fine dining establishment—he should have stolen the tablecloth but the napkin would do. In the nick of time he reached into his breast pocket, and with both arms acting as his chute lines, deployed the massive eight-inch square napkin emblazoned with the Vatican logo. He screeched to a halt and, like a feather, gently floated to the ground. Except Ciro, outside of his delusional vision, didn't steal a napkin, and Ciro knew a napkin wouldn't actually have helped, even if he had been so resourceful. No, he knew that with or without napkin, he splattered. He was despondent.

His mind's pain encompassed him in misery. His subconscious brought on another vision. Suddenly he envisioned himself on a dark tower, alone, no judge, no prosecutor, no jury, no witnesses, and no defense. He was hardly a gunslinger; he was the owner of One Fire, not a firestarter, and now he was stranded in this dead zone that carried a shining, bouncing, mind-devouring wheel.

When he was awake—and those waking interludes were becoming more frequent—he fought hard to communicate. He was desperate to, and his mind shrieked, was seared by anguish. He wasn't sure who the new doctor was, though he felt that he recognized the voice. Ciro wasn't sure if she was American, Canadian, English, Australian, or perhaps another nationality; he didn't understand a word the English-speaking doctor had said, but he fully understood the translation. He wished he could slip back into another dream but he had no command of his waking or dreaming mind.

He had dreamed about his family, about Ote, other friends, old girlfriends, and soccer. He dreamed most often of Amalia. He could hear her crying; the doctor hadn't offered up much hope. His father was crying. His mother completed the weeping trio.

"We don't have the knowledge to make this decision," Lucio complained, "and how can she possibly burden us with this? Maybe she is a great doctor, but I don't like her holier than thou attitude. I'm not sure if it's because she's an American or a doctor, but I don't like it either way."

"All of us need to regain our composure for Ciro's sake," Amalia said through sobs. "Think of Ciro for a moment instead of yourselves—please, it's so important!"

Ciro had found it comforting to hear Amalia and his parents. He had gradually learned his greatest joy was when he could smell Amalia. But overhearing this conversation was like having his teeth pulled out with a pair of vice grips.

"Let's bring in Ote," Amalia continued. "No one knows him better! He would know what Ciro would want!"

Ote's heart dropped when he was summoned. He did not want to see his friend like this. He had been at the hospital every day but one, yet had never entered this room. Now that he had finally crossed the threshold, he tried not to look at his friend. These were not memories he wanted.

Signore Pane's summation of Angela's remarks was brief and to the point. Then he asked, simply, "What would Ciro want?"

After several minutes of internal debate, Ote answered. "Ciro would know that he didn't know the answer. He would listen to those who did—he would listen to the doctor."

It was true. Ciro was a very pragmatic man.

In Ciro's dream, he could see Amalia crying as she came near to him. Ote was by his side as always; the priest was there, all of his family was there, and they were all crying. Even Ote was crying, and vaguely it occurred to Ciro that he had never seen his friend cry before. All the while Ciro seemed to be floating, growing increasingly happy as he floated, and feeling as though he had never been happier. *Why do they cry when I am so happy?* he asked himself.

After the social worker left, Lucio informed Angela of their decision. She knew how difficult it must have been, placing all of your trust in a so-called expert, an American woman no less. She imagined that it was Amalia who had won out. Amalia had always known her as a tourist, but she knew her nonetheless.

Angela arrived fifteen minutes later with Dr. Natale, a pulmonologist and the hospital's chief of staff. They invited everyone who wished to be in the room to spend a little time with Ciro. They advised that the procedure was routine and would take no more than fifteen minutes.

Everyone present knew of the revised orders indicating the wish not to resuscitate. When the doctors entered the room, the onlookers were all in prayer. Ote and his wife held Amalia. Ciro's sister, Isabella, was in her parents' arms while aunts and uncles held cousins. None were prepared or composed as they prayed. Some consoled themselves with the belief that he had already died back on the beach at La Praia, that that was where he would have wanted to die.

Father Viglianti was there, at the family's request—indeed, it was their only condition that he was to remain with Ciro and perform The Anointing of the Sick while the doctors performed their duties.

Back in dream, Ciro's mind was once again peaceful. He was in the basilica, feeling it almost as though it were heaven on earth, yet everyone persisted in their crying. He was mystified by the emotions of those around him, as he was void of any pain for the first time in forever. He was filled with joy, softened and awed with almighty reverence.

No one outside of Ciro's room heard his hospital door open; no one knew how much time had elapsed since Angela, the pulmonologist, and Father Viglianti had evicted them from Ciro's room for the removal of his breathing tube. Time had assumed a raw, tender quality.

Viglianti stood before them with tears running down his face. He extended his arms to Ciro's parents. Amalia was the first to collapse as the glance she exchanged with Viglianti shredded what remained of her heart. After weeks of interminable strain, reality had finally defeated faith, bringing her to the ground beneath its unbearable weight.

While dreaming, Ciro realized what was happening. He began to cry along with all those surrounding him. It was the defining moment of his life. Amalia was striding like an angel down the aisle to make him hers.

In a flowing white gown she drifted toward him, tears flying back from her face, and strangely it was Ote's father who accompanied her—no, wait, it was her father, though he couldn't be sure. Everyone in attendance was standing, drawing closer and closer to Ciro, an organist triumphing their arrival and the music growing louder as his angel neared.

Chapter 11: You Whirling Wheel

"Aprajita!"

She turned. Piccadilly was always crowded—at night the lights resembled a less vulgar Vegas. Alessio! Alessio? Yes, yes, it was him. But how? Here in London! Had he been looking for her? Had someone told him the truth?

She felt a nervous happiness and guilt simultaneously. She had often thought she should have reached out to him, given him a chance. At the very least, send a cowardly letter and await a reply without expectation. She quickly searched her mind before opting to put on a mask.

"Aprajita, I'm delighted to see you!"

"Hi! How are you?" She would pretend that she couldn't remember his name.

He didn't answer her question, instead noting the baby in the stroller. "Are congratulations in order?"

"Congratulations? I don't understand."

"Your baby!" he exclaimed.

"Oh, this isn't my baby. I'm here serving as a nanny for an executive I work for!" She looked at him and frowned. "I'm embarrassed that I can't place your name. Still a little jetlagged, I suppose."

He did his best to hide his dejection. "Alessio! I was in India two and a half years ago at Havikiran. I worked with Romil on a project!"

"Ah, yes, yes of course, so good to see you. Are you in London long?"

"Came in for Wimbledon, here about a week. I wanted to ask you about Romil, how he's doing. I expected to see his sons playing here by now!"

She laughed. "Not yet, I think that maybe they're still a

little young, as far as I know. I don't work with him often."

Alessio was looking intently at the baby and computing some simple math in his head.

"What's the baby's name? Is it a boy or a girl? How old?"

She opened her mouth to reply but he interrupted her.

"Around fifteen months?"

"Well, let's see, I think Ramesh had a birthday a few months back. That would put him around fifteen months. Such a good guess!"

The look he gave her almost robbed her of her breath.

"It wasn't a guess, Aprajita."

Aprajita stuck to her story. "I'm not sure that I understand."

Alessio was at a loss for words. He wanted to run, he wanted to hold her, but most of all he was unbalanced by this truth. He was generally not fond of the truth and tended to avoid it. It was what confused him the most and it was a jolting, displeasing revelation.

Why hadn't he been informed? Had someone else taken over his role as the child's father? Was it some sixth sense that had tormented him with visions of Aprajita for the past few years? How could he have feelings for her anyway? He didn't really even know her—so he kept telling himself, and had been telling himself for the past two years.

"I find it difficult to believe that by happenstance I stand here with the knowledge that I have a son and that you found it necessary to say not a single word affirming this to me. To this moment you choose to deny me. Do you find me a monster?"

She had never considered him the monster—now *she* felt, intensely, like the monster. "How are you so sure?" was the she could assemble in the moment. No longer able to mask her throbbing emotions, her mouth quivered with the question.

Alessio was relieved to hear this. He imagined that she would try to continue with her masquerade and excuse herself or call for help. When one's own mother has denied you, you have a propensity to expect rejection.

He bent down and held his son in his arms for the first time, an instantaneous love for his child overpowering him, drowning all of his other feelings in that moment. And for the first time, Aprajita saw his essence, his real self.

"Perhaps we should go to my flat," she said. "We need to talk." She felt relieved, for a burden had been lifted from her. Although it was true that she still didn't really know Alessio, her presumptions of him had suddenly been shattered like a crystal vase hurled against a wall.

"Excuse me," he said. "I just need to return to the restaurant to pay the bill. Please wait for me here because we do need to talk."

He carried his son into the restaurant, fearing that if he relinquished him to his mother she would escape into the night. Ashley's mouth dropped as he walked in with the baby in his arms.

"Ladies!" he boomed, "I just discovered that I'm a father! I beg your pardon and thank you for a wonderful evening. I do hope you understand, crazy as it is."

With that he tossed five hundred pounds on the table before them, not bothering to check the bill. He gave them each a quick Italian peck on each side of their faces and with that bid them *arrivederci!*

Alessio and Aprajita walked to her home in silence down the bustling streets of Piccadilly, Alessio still cradling his son. His walk was full of life, while Aprajita couldn't shake her feelings of guilt and remorse. She was struck by the metaphoric parallel between the empty stroller she pushed and her heart.

"Here we are," she said when they arrived at her building. Ramesh was now sleeping in his father's arms. Alessio liked the ring of "we," how it left her lips so easily.

"Will I meet your husband or boyfriend?" he tried to joke, surprised by his awkwardness. They were two years removed from a month-long affair that lacked any real substance, and he was utterly clueless as to what might come next. For the moment, he simply relished the time holding his sleeping son.

"My husband is away on business, but that doesn't mean that I'm not faithful to him!"

Alessio's heart shrank.

She laughed. "You were my last—who wants a single mother toting a baby?"

The relief in his face disarmed Aprajita. She would never have imagined that he would tolerate, much less be eager for, a family.

Her studio was small, perhaps one hundred and fifty square meters. You entered through the kitchen, with a minifridge, washing machine, and small oven all along one wall. Three large windows, bare of curtains, let in light from the outside. A red loveseat sat next to a small black kitchen table on wheels. There were toys scattered about, and an infant's high chair stood in the corner. A single folding chair completed the décor. There were two doors leading from the room— presumably one for the bedroom and one for the bath. Alessio opened one and then other and saw Ramesh's crib next to Aprajita's bed. With the organic motion of an experienced father, he tenderly lay Ramesh down.

"Can I get a drink? You like gin and tonic, don't you?"

"How is it that you remember my drink but not my name?"

"Oh, that wasn't quite true—I think of your name every day!" She opened a cabinet door. "And by the way, I don't have any gin. How about—let's see—orange juice?"

She handed him a glass and they stood there, neither making a move to sit down, each maintaining their space and continuing to appraise the situation. Then Alessio heard the sound of Ramesh's cry for the first time. Strangely, he rather enjoyed it. As starkly foreign as the entire situation was to anything he had experienced before in his life, he felt composed. He moved and thought as though in a dream, yet a dream steeped in the most delicious reality.

"He's wet his diaper—would you like to change it?"

"I'd love to, but I don't think that I know how!"

Aprajita wagged her finger at him, motioning him into the bedroom. There was a changing table he hadn't noticed piled with diapers, creams, Wet Ones, and other assorted baby care supplies. It was totally surreal—an hour ago, he was on the verge of another successful conquest (two, in fact), and the next thing he knew he was changing his son's diaper. He wondered if there might be more baby Alessios elsewhere in the world.

With the diaper successfully changed, he was the first to sit, settling into the folding chair and sipping his orange juice. He wondered if he might awake from this magnificent dream. He wasn't sure what the future with Aprajita might hold, but he was now a father. Alessio needed this more than anything, more than anything he could have ever imagined he might ever need.

Neither knew what to say. The silence was broken by Alessio.

"So what's an apartment like this run, if you don't mind my asking?"

Aprajita looked relieved by this offer to small talk.

"All utilities paid, mostly furnished, no car park, and a good deal at one thousand eight hundred pounds monthly. Would you like to see some pictures of Ramesh?"

"Of course I would!"

She opened a kitchen cupboard and removed three shoeboxes overflowing with photos.

"Looks like you're due for more shoes soon!" Alessio joked.

It took a couple of hours to get through the photos, for Aprajita had a story to go along with each. To Alessio the time flew by. Viewing the photos softened the tension, and they became more and more comfortable with one another as they gazed at pictures of their son.

"It must be very difficult for you."

Aprajita had already told him about his daycare, his trips to the parks, his first steps, and his first words, almost every detail documented by photograph.

"We get by, and the joy outweighs the difficulty, always."

Alessio understood this. He had grown to love Ramesh in the span of only a few hours. He knew without any doubt that he would throw himself in front of one of London's red buses to save him. His son gave him a purpose. Maybe his family would forgive him when he introduced Ramesh to his mother, when he showed her that she was a grandmother. Certainly she couldn't blame an infant for the acts of his father.

It was early Monday morning by now. Alessio had accepted that Aprajita would not run off and hide, though they had never really had their talk. He thought that it was best to postpone it.

"I'm staying just up the road at the May Fair. Would you like to meet me for breakfast at the hotel?"

"Ramesh wakes early—would seven be okay?"

"I'll send a car over at five minutes till seven. Can we make a day of it? Maybe you two can show me around?"

"I took the day off so that you can spend time with Ramesh. Alessio, I'm so sorry that I never tried to reach you. Every time I thought to do so, which was very often, I talked myself out it. I was scared, I didn't know how you would react. I loved your love but it vanished after just one month. How could I burden you? I didn't mean for it to happen, you must believe me! I thought we were protected but something failed."

She lowered her head, her eyes shining. "I'm sorry that I pretended not to remember your name. Of course I know that he's your child, there were no others. Ramesh has brought me such joy, and now that I see the joy he brings you I feel terrible. I am so sorry, I hope that you will forgive me one day.

I'll never keep him from you again. I couldn't.'"

"It's a miracle for us both," Alessio said tenderly. "You didn't know that I felt the same way. I understand how you feel. I think of you often—it's so true!"

He stared intently into her eyes, trying to impress the truth upon her, and surprising himself that he could have a truth to convey.

"Let's not point fingers. We spent just a short time together. And I never reached out; I could have easily found you through your work. I didn't because I feared you would reject me. You would have had to work hard to find me, that I know. It was a miracle that you walked by the restaurant where I was eating and that I saw you—a miracle! It must be! I want to spend time with my son, yes, and I want to spend time with you."

He saw her expression and hastened to clarify. "Not like before. Not sex. I want real time together. When we first met we always did what I wanted to do. Now I want to do what *you* want to do. What better way to get to know someone than to do what they do every day?"

Alessio amazed even himself with this spontaneous, heartfelt barrage of emotions and words. But he knew that he meant it—somehow knowing that he would always have Ramesh gave him the confidence to expose himself without any hesitation.

With glistening eyes, Aprajita stroked his face.

"I'll see you tomorrow. Thank you so much for your words. I'm so happy that this miracle, as you call it, has brought you to your son. He needs you!"

Halfway on Alessio's walk back to his hotel, his iPhone twinkled. He saw that it was line two and felt a cold wave of dread. He steeled himself and answered the phone.

"*Pronto ... si ... si ... si ... si.*" As he listened intently, he quickly scribbled the encrypted message onto his notepad. When the conversation ended, he was extremely relieved that his vacation would not be interrupted, that he could spend time with Aprajita and their son tomorrow. His anonymous boss's only requirement was that Alessio make a phone call to an unknown recipient and pass along an incredibly vague message. Most of his assignments were of this nature, generally completed in five minutes or less.

He phoned his source as instructed and passed along the message. The voice on the other end always answered his phone too, no matter the time. Another grinding day at the office for Alessio, he thought, though his source indicated, as coincidence would have it, that Alessio should prepare for a return trip to India. He knew that he was involved in some sort of underworld, and as adept as he was about erasing horrific memories from his mind, deep within he knew the truth.

Chapter 12: Fate Strikes Down the Strong Man

Romil's large extended family always spent a summer month in Assagao in the Indian state of Goa. His two sisters, the middle children, his brother, and their spouses had all moved to the United States years ago to go to college. Romil, the eldest, was the only one to return home.

His siblings, all physicians living along the East Coast, saw each other often, but they only returned to their homeland once a year. It was a much-anticipated time for their children to spend with their grandparents, their uncle, and their ten cousins.

Romil's father had added a separate detached villa that contained three large bedrooms, each with four beds and three bathrooms. The children took over this boarding house, which looked out over a large infinity pool. The entire estate was surrounded by tropical gardens, with palm and fig trees taking center stage. And the beautiful white-sand North Goa beach on the Arabian Sea was just a short path away. Romil's parents enjoyed this retreat for half of every year, but it was when the entire family reunited that this property was truly transformed into its rightful existence.

As grand as the property was, it was the joy continually shared here by the close family that was even grander. They were rich, not just in terms of their possessions, but through their love. Their summer month always saw the home and grounds filled with laughter, relaxation, and energy.

The Bahls were in their first week of reacquainting. Romil and his siblings had demanding, stressful careers, but here there were no worries, no disruptive phone calls. They used this time to rejuvenate, to purge their minds of a year's worth of clutter.

They genuinely loved one another and enjoyed recollections of their childhood. Their spouses mischievously probed for stories about their significant others that they could leverage to their advantage later. That such a large, diverse group had gathered here for years without one incident of jealous envy was remarkable. No off-handed remarks meant to harm another. They demonstrated dignity and integrity, but above all it was their love of life that defined them, and they were pleased to share this love with anyone. Even the staff enjoyed the family reunion time more than any other time of the year, despite the added pressures that came with maintaining a household of nineteen. Needless to say, with so many beachgoers the sand was everywhere.

Breakfast and lunch was always served at the house, and most dinners too, making for a hot tub–sized sink full of dishes. Add laundry and this made for a very busy day for the staff. But they were happy to do the work, for the love here was contagious.

This evening they dined in the nearby community of Panjim. Their huge table was filled to capacity with smiles. Romil enjoyed his roasted nutmeg chicken with potatoes and peppers. The children sat at the end of the table but Romil could hear Vijay and Guhan boasting of their tennis victories, which he disapprovingly found lacking in humility. He made a note to discuss this with them privately while sipping a frozen daiquiri made of apricot, tequila, and honey. It was refreshing on this humid summer night.

As the family stood up to depart, Vijay snatched his father's mostly empty cocktail and slipped into the shadows. The engaging, encouraging discussions continued as Romil's father paid the tab before they walked back to the comforts of the compound.

The sun was setting over the Arabian Sea as they gathered in the courtyard. Romil's father was telling a story to his grandchildren about a time when Romil was fifteen. Romil and his siblings shared a wonderful childhood and the patriarch conveyed it eloquently, though not necessarily accurately. Romil's wife, Shalini, was seated next to him as their boys were sitting cross-legged at his feet and listening intently to their grandpa.

"Romil, I heard your speech to Vijay and Guhan on our walk home about humility and while I agree with your intent, there's something to be said about encouraging confidence and effort too. I remember when you were their age and had just won the regional science bowl and how you paraded around the house holding your trophy above your arms. You worked hard to win that bowl and your mother and I only smiled as you boasted. Why not boast a little when it's deserved?"

Before Romil could answer, Vijay jumped up and raised his arms as if in celebration. The entire gathering cheered him on, even Romil, as Vijay strutted along the deck. Then he staggered and fell into the pool.

The laughing grew louder as Vijay thrashed in the pool like a hooked mackerel attempting to escape. His limbs splashed wildly until he went motionless with arms and legs spread wide, facedown in the pool.

"Okay, Vijay, that's enough. You made your point!"

"Vijay!"

"Vijay!"

But there was no reply. Romil dived in to rescue his son. Upon reaching him he was horrified to discover that his son was completely unresponsive.

"Somebody help me get him out of here—he's not playing!"

Romil pulled his son to the pool's edge and Shalini and Guhan pulled Vijay's limp, wet body from the pool. His eyes were vacant, lifeless.

One of Romil's sisters kneeled next to Vijay and checked his vitals. Then she ripped off his shirt and started performing CPR on him. "Call an ambulance!"

As Romil pulled himself from the pool, he was starting to feel dizzy, nauseous, and anxious. His heart was racing furiously; it felt as though it might jump right out of his chest.

Anxiety turned to terror as he saw his entire family huddled around Vijay's sprawled body. Romil's vision was blurring. He balanced himself by grabbing his wife's shaking shoulder.

My God, he thought, *I'm having a heart attack.* His brother noticed the distress on his face and ran to him just as he collapsed beside his son near the pool's edge.

Romil's brother checked his pulse—it was nearing two hundred and fifty beats per minute. Romil realized the gravity of his situation and gazed around the room, now strangely at peace. "I love you all!" he exclaimed.

"Call an ambulance!" his brother shouted.

His face twisted, eyes begging, Romil reached for his wife. Then his eyes rolled back and his arms and legs shook as if he was having a seizure.

Chaos ensued. The families' shrieks of dismay could be heard from the beach.

Shalini and Guhan stood back while Romil's brother and sister did what they could. Shalini was in shock, with a dazed, almost expressionless look of disbelief, but her arms trembled as she held onto Guhan.

Romil and Vijay never said another word. They died there among their family in their favorite place at their favorite time before the ambulance arrived, as their medically trained relatives struggled vainly to save them. No doctor in the world could have undone the lethal droplet of the drug known in the lab as a mixture of Ramipril, epinephrine, lisinopril, intra gastro, integrilin, & oxy neosynephrine. It was a complex name, always abbreviated on the street. It only took a tiny drop.

This nanotoxin was undetectable and there were no antidotes. An autopsy would reveal only a sudden myocardial infarction. There'd be no doubt by the family that Vijay must have been born with a bad heart and the trauma of this evening had triggered Romil's instant death as well.

It had been their assassin's method of execution for many years, though he envied the pleasure that his predecessors enjoyed back in the good old days that weren't really that long ago. The assassin's favorite way to punish the accused, taken from the history books he had read, was the dismemberment by weight method. The accused straddled an elevated maul with arms bound up, but with the necessary slack, his dangling ankles fitted with chains that swung so that heavy weights could be attached to dangle beneath. The executioners added additional weight slowly and with pleasure until the accused would literally be ripped in half to the delight of the masses gathered below. By brutally dismembering a sinner in a public forum for all to witness, the audience who watched the accused scream in agony were inevitably much less likely to transgress in similar manner.

The tragic event, thought to have been an act of God, changed the entire dynamic of the surviving Bahls. They sold the vacation home immediately, and their smiles, joy, and happiness would be diminished for the rest of their lives.

Chapter 13: Then Soothes

As his unconscious mind floated effortlessly from thought to thought, Ciro listened to the most perfect words. He had heard them before, though never addressed to him. Father Viglianti stood before him as Ciro gripped his earthly angel's hand.

"Dearly beloved, we are gathered here, in this site of God and in the presence of these witnesses, to join Ciro and Amalia in holy matrimony, which is an honorable estate instituted of God in the time of man's innocence and signifies to us the mystical union between Christ and His Church ..."

A thrilled Ciro turned to face those gathered, and with a huge grin raised his arm in triumph. He slapped Ote with a jubilant thud on his back, causing his friend to lunge forward and nearly lose his balance. Ote had needed the courage of a few drinks to stand before all these people, perhaps too many drinks.

And his dream again faded.

Outside Ciro's room, Viglianti recognized that his tears and demeanor had been misconstrued. The person who most needed to hear his news had passed out. She was lying prone on the hospital's floor and was being tended to by Ote and Juliana.

"He made it through! He's breathing on his own! There is still hope for his life!"

The pendulum of emotions swung swiftly from utter despondency to irrepressible joy. When Amalia awoke, Ote was quick to relay the priest's message: "He made it through! He's breathing on his own!"

Amalia immediately rushed to Ciro, who remained unconscious. His parents and sister greeted her with loving hugs, tears of joy still streaming down their faces.

"I knew you would make it, Ciro," she said. "You must continue to fight! So many love you—please don't ever give up!"

She had grown into the habit of talking to Ciro only when they were alone. She'd worried they might consider it crazy to talk to someone in a coma. But after the ordeal of believing he had died, she no longer cared what the others thought.

"If we could only communicate with you," she added, "I know you would never give up!"

No one had realized, but not only Ciro could listen, he *was* able to communicate in return. His nurses, doctors, family, and Amalia had all missed his subtle messages. His heart rate quickened whenever the doctors discussed his condition. Any interruption or turmoil in his room encouraged a similar increase in his heart rate. When Amalia or his family comforted him, his heart rate dropped. Ciro had always communicated with his heart, and the coma he was in made no difference.

Without the tube in his mouth, he looked like Ciro for the first time in weeks. This change in appearance alone comforted Amalia and Ciro's family.

Angela joined them in Ciro's room thirty minutes later. Hope, she knew, was dangerously complex. Tempering hope was a tricky undertaking. It was made more difficult by the language and cultural barriers she faced. But the truth remained her ally.

"I am very pleased that Ciro's brain stem remains viable. This was demonstrated by his ability to breathe on his own. Prior to the removal of his breathing tube we deflated his endotracheal tube cuff and he responded very well. We removed the tube and suctioned his airways and applied this nasal cannula, which provides supplemental oxygen. I'm going to let him rest today, though I will test his blood gases and take an x-ray to make sure his lungs aren't filling with fluids. We'll resume feedings in a couple hours. I'm decreasing his dopamine drip, which had helped to maintain his blood pressure. I already canceled his orders for the Propofol that had kept him sedated. Under sedation, the prior EGG results are worthless.

"Tomorrow we are going to challenge him and start physical therapy. The therapists will stimulate his arms and legs with range of motion exercises to reduce the muscular atrophy that is already establishing. We still don't know the extent of the impact to his cerebral cortex so we have no way of predicting his final outcome. I will know more once we do an electro-encephalogram while he's under no sedatives, so don't be alarmed when you see many probes glued to his head for the next twenty-four hours. And try not to be alarmed by the smell; the glue used to attach the wires stinks quite a bit. We will test him with probe lights in his eyes to see if that triggers seizures. We hope that it won't. We'll give him a set of commands: open your eyes, squeeze my hand, wiggle your toes. I will have Amalia talk to him. We doubt he'll follow any of these commands, but we want to see if there's a change in brain activity. See if anything stimulates him and at what level. I'll have a much clearer understanding with these results. Remain hopeful and continue to pray, but Ciro's battle has just begun."

What pleased Ciro's family and Amalia the most was that the doctor had referred to Ciro's future for the first time. Much of the medical jargon had eluded them, but they were as buoyant as they could be with this newfound promise of hope.

Angela wasn't picturing herself in her new villa quite yet, but she and her husband had viewed their options from the road after she had returned from her first day as Ciro's attending physician. From the outside, they were leaning toward the villa painted in a salmon hue. She wondered whether they would arrive at the point where they could make their selection based on an inspection of all the properties, inside and out.

Once Gio's helicopter landed her back at the San Pietro, she phoned the billionaire with an update. She didn't disclose private patient data, given her scanty understanding of Italy's privacy laws. Her update to Gio was simple: "I am pleased with his progress, but the brain is very complex. Some get better, others worse. Time will tell."

Like most successful doctors, Angela was able to leave her work behind her, easing her mind from the burdens of the past days to join her husband at the pool. He didn't ask her about Ciro's condition, as he too was a former healthcare provider and all too familiar with the tendency to bring burdens home. They both intended to enjoy their free time though Todd might argue that his wife was prone, on occasion or two, to outbursts that he had always attributed to the stress of her job.

Ciro awoke, so to speak, and heard his mother, father, sister, and Amalia speaking with more hope in their voices. He was less groggy now. His heart rate dropped as he listened. This went unnoticed as always. Their words touched him and caressed him. His loathing of his predicament and his inability to communicate were momentarily eased by their words.

He accepted that, for now, this was the way it had to be. They were talking about what a good friend Ote had been throughout the ordeal. They thought it would be best to invite him to Gio's apartment. *Who is Gio?* The only Gio Ciro knew was the rich guy who owned everything.

"I'm still in shock that Gio took the time to help," Amalia said. "I don't know anyone who knows him. Ciro never mentioned him, even when he would be seen around the coast, driving his fancy sports car."

"It was Father Viglianti who spoke with him," said Lucio. "They are friends somehow, likely through the church. He never goes to Mass, though. Maybe the father conducts Mass privately for him?"

"And Dr. Neurmer has been so good," Amalia said. "Ciro always liked her. He's known her forever but no one knew she was a doctor. Ciro thought she was a chief of some sort. I'm so glad they got rid of that nasty doctor before her!"

Ciro drifted back to sleep, easing softly into a dream about the first time he had met Todd and Angela. Ciro could barely comprehend "hello" in English at that age. Their words were foreign but their actions easily translated into Italian. It was the first summer Ciro captained a boat on his own and he was smiling as much as the American couple. They wanted to go to Capri to see the Blue Grotto but somehow without words Ciro convinced them to go to the closer Emerald Grotto, then to the Gali islands for snorkeling, then to a wonderful restaurant accessible only by boat, rather than waste the day traveling to Capri. It was *his* route, and a good one. The American couple spent their entire time awestruck. Ciro took hundreds of photos of them. Every hundred yards or so, they wanted a picture in front of a different background.

At lunch, they were able to communicate; their waiter spoke a little English and was happy to translate. They told the waiter to express their great gratitude for this wonderful experience. Ciro truthfully replied that this had been the most fun he'd ever had captaining a boat, though he failed to mention he had only just started captaining.

They spent the rest of the day in and around the waters of Positano and Praiano. The Americans had sipped wine all day, which only enhanced the pleasure they took in the surroundings. They got a little frisky as the sun was starting to set. Ciro had looked away, embarrassed and blushing when he noticed Todd slipping his hand inside his wife's bikini bottoms.

Ote was sitting in his very familiar seat outside Ciro's room, a pastel blue plastic chair with a chrome-plated frame. There were seven such seats attached together with no armrests, not entirely dissimilar to those airport seats near departure gates. For the first time he realized how uncomfortable they were.

Now he knew why his butt was sore—for the last few

weeks he had slept in this chair, cried in it, and contemplated in it. He had even forgotten that he was a smoker—two weeks had passed without a cigarette and he had never even realized it. More surprising, no one else had noticed either. Their minds were elsewhere.

With the shock of the day over, Ote tried to bring order to his scattered thoughts and emotions. In spite of his efforts, his mind still raced from one thing to another. Should he move it to a better hiding spot and risk discovery, or leave it in the current hiding place? Ciro, his voice of reason, would advise him to determine the greater risk and act accordingly.

Before Ciro opened One Fire, he studied all of this financial stuff—the cost to operate and maintain his boat, the price of the space and the cost to renovate it, the projected revenues and projected expenses—that he calmly pored over and then just as calmly and decisively decided to open it.

Ote had simply thought it was a good idea—a beach club! That makes sense. He hadn't cared how much the sun loungers cost or how to set the rate the customers would pay to lounge in them. That they'd want somewhere to lounge was all that mattered to him. Ciro determined the menu by the cost of goods, the labor to prepare, and the cost to buy the kitchen equipment and maintain it. To Ote, the customers would be hungry, so they would feed them.

As he was considering this, his mind began to drift again as it usually did. Ote, who also knew of Gio yet didn't *know* Gio, had much greater respect for the man he had never really given much thought to before his intervention on behalf of a person he didn't even know.

Gio didn't interact with the locals, at least not those in Ote's crowd. Ote hoped that he would get a chance to one day thank him, return the gift in some way. The €50,000 Gio had given to the Pane's remained a secret; all Ote knew was that he had made his apartment available and had hired the American doctor.

Amalia sat beside Ote without his realizing she was there. She presumed he was thinking of Ciro and didn't interrupt him until Ote turned to her and smiled.

"Hey, we are all going to the apartment for lunch," she said. "Join us! It will do us all good to get away."

The Panes and Amalia had conspired to return Ote to his family, get him back to work and his routine. He was at least cleaner now than he had been, but his dull, unhealthy appearance persisted. His zest for life was seemingly extinguished.

Gio's apartment in Naples was a twenty-minute drive from the hospital. A quarter-mile from the sea, the apartment was nestled in the historic section of the city. Ote wasn't surprised that the apartment was a luxurious penthouse. He walked out onto the terrace, a massive structure tiled in blue majolica with a wisp of white lightly brushed onto each segment.

It was the sea and Mt. Vesuvius that drew Ote's attention. Would the sea, their domain for all these years and the scene of so many classic tales, look the same to him if Ciro died?

He remembered when they were ten, how they were both intrigued by Vesuvius after a school field trip. All of his classmates were. Back then they would pretend that it erupted. Lava all the way to Praiano, smoke everywhere; they could barely breathe, they had to save the city, had to avoid the lava and dust.

They saw Vesuvius rumbling and they knew they had to offer the gods a girl. Usually they'd choose Ina Collina, the snitch, as their sacrifice. Of course, she didn't actually play with them—they might use a broom to play the role of Ina and envision her in its place.

Too bad they hadn't been videotaped during this play— their prayers to the gods in the offering were hilarious. The prayers of most ten-year-olds are funny, though hardly that much more ludicrous than other prayers.

They would passionately argue over who would play the role of the villainous hero and throw Ina Collina into the fiery volcano. They struggled with the broom, imitating a fight with their sacrificial maiden, dragging the broom to the volcano's edge.

This was usually where the real struggle began as Ote and Ciro fought, vying to be the one who tossed Ina to the gods, mitigating their wrath and causing Vesuvius to go dormant and saving the village of Pompeii.

What fun a ten-year-old has with only his imagination. They were not afraid to imagine, to dream. They didn't know any better.

"Ote, are you alright?" Lucio startled him from his reminiscence.

"I was just thinking about the time—"

"Maria caught you boys smoking pot?" Lucio cut him off with a smirk.

"I *did* think of that the other day, but more about the pain our parents caused us. I got kicked off the soccer team!"

"I'm surprised you could remember anything through that haze!"

"I remember when we found a big joint in your car and smoked it. It was especially fun watching you try to remember what you had done with it!"

"I remember that—you boys were wicked but I learned. You never found another one did you?"

"We figured you forgot you smoked dope!"

Much of Lucio's sensible behavior was innate, a genetic inheritance that had been nurtured since his earliest youth. He was an attorney trained at the prestigious Pontificia Università della Santa Croce in Rome. He could have moved his young family anywhere, but declined job offers of that would have made him wealthy. Instead he remained in his hometown of Praiano set up a modest practice that had provided more for his family than a swelling bank account.

Lucio was only twenty years older than his son and Ote and an active father. The scuffs on his soccer ball showed that he still maintained his love of the sport, a passion he enjoyed sharing with his son and Ote. There were a few hiccups along the way when a father had to be a father, but overall the time they'd shared was cheerful.

"Deep in my heart I know that Ciro will make it," Lucio said. "I cannot explain it but, even today, when all seemed lost, I remained confident. Ciro has a strong spirit, and he has not yet discovered the joy of a child as we have. Soon he will recover."

Lucio put his hand on Ote's shoulder. "My family is so grateful to you. We have been touched by how you've guarded over Ciro, and we understand more than anyone why you do it. You have always been by his side. But be by his side when he needs you most—once he recovers. You must save your strength for this time. For now, show your love to your family. Return to work, resume your life. Amalia, Maria, and I will stand watch. I told the same to Isabella just today. You know that Ciro would tell you the same!"

Ote was about to protest, but Lucio's last words convinced him. In his mind he could hear Ciro say, "*Vai a casa!*"

"After lunch, I wish to speak to him privately," said Ote. "I want to encourage him and thank him for his friendship. I want to tell him good-bye before I go."

Ote bent his head and cried. Lucio embraced his second son, Ciro's twin. "All will be well, Ote. Soon Ciro will greet you and thank you for your friendship."

Following lunch and a tour of Gio's apartment, they returned to the hospital. On the drive, Ote wondered what he would say to his best friend, although mostly he prayed that it wouldn't be the last time he saw him alive.

Ote was apprehensive as he entered Ciro's room. His friend, always alive with boundless energy, now lay dormant on the bed. Ote fought back a sudden rush of sadness and took Ciro's hand.

"Do you remember the time I climbed the mountain across from Il Germano? You told me I was foolish to try but I did it anyway. Halfway up I got stuck on the side of the cliff. I was paralyzed by fear, unable to retreat or continue. I could barely hear you, but you patiently and deliberately gave me confidence to finish my climb. You noted that the easiest part was a mere five meters away, and you guided me around my impasse. I wish that I could guide you around yours, but I am not smart like you. Listen to yourself, Ciro, and guide yourself back to us. I struggle in the dark without you.

"You have been a true friend forever. You overlooked my faults, you forgave me often. I would get us in trouble, and you would get us out of it. I would fly off the hook, and you would calm me. I am undeserving of your friendship but you have never wavered, a constant loving friend always.

"I have to return to Praiano, return to my family, return to work. You have to rest and heal. I know that you will. I know your will. For now, good-bye, dear friend. I pray that soon we will be fishing, cheering on the *Partenopei*, and arguing as we always have."

Ote spent the next several minutes holding Ciro's hand, his mouth contorting in a futile effort not to sob.

Ciro was keenly aware now. This awareness was less unbearable than it had felt before. He was awake more often now, though time still eluded him. It was the first time he had heard Ote's voice.

He remembered well when Ote was trapped on the side of that mountain. He remembered how they laughed when he finally made it up. The moment was fodder for weeks of teasing. In his mind, Ciro smiled throughout Ote's retelling. If Ote had known he was eavesdropping, it was unlikely he would have been so vulnerable.

Ciro had never heard Ote speak from his heart before. He

doubted whether even Juliana had heard an unfiltered Ote. He had never heard him cry, not even when his father died. His puffy red eyes were evidence that he cried, but he never did so in front of him.

Ciro was deeply impressed by his friend's inspirational message. He likened his predicament to being stuck on the side of the mountain, just as Ote had intended. He strained to take the bold first step.

The next morning the EEG technician wended through Ciro's curly black hair and began the tedious process of gluing the silver aspirin-sized probes to Ciro's scalp and taping them down into fine rows. A crayon box of colored leads was attached to each, exiting through a stocking cap meant to hold everything in place. Ciro heard a new male voice, the raspy voice of heavy smoker. The man wasn't saying much, just your occasional "*Cazzo!*"

Ciro guessed that he was about to undergo the tests that everyone had been talking about earlier. The vapors from glue attaching the probes to his scalp were mind-numbingly revolting. He preferred the sterile chlorine-infused old poop scent that normally permeated his nostrils to this new disturbing smell and wished that he could hold his nose. He longed for the scent of the sea, flowers, fish, his house, even his old shoes, but mostly for the scent of Amalia.

Amalia and Maria had observed this entire process a few days ago. This time they watched with greater hope. Angela had told them earlier that it made no sense to conduct the test on a sedated patient. She walked in just as the technician completed the system integrity test and asked Amalia and Maria to step out of the room for a moment.

"The strobe is very bright, like a welder's arc, and can potentially cause seizures in anyone who views it."

"He is showing promising waves," Angela told the technician after they left. "Between two and three per second!"

Ciro was dreaming again. Amalia was wearing his favorite

cream-colored bikini, the naughty one. All the men on the beach were staring at her tanned, toned body. He saw them looking and with pride swelling his chest, he smiled in reply.

They were taking their time entering the cooler spring sea on the beach of Arienzo, one of their favorite places to sneak off to, even now that his One Fire was in competition with it. Taking your time there was encouraged. The umbrellas and sun loungers were of the blue variety, but the craggy rockcrop surroundings were the same.

While holding hands they hurried to get off the hot pebbles that formed the beach and plunged their feet into the soothing sea.

"Ah, my Amalia, this water it makes me shake, like my heart does when you are near!"

They inched farther into the sea, adjusting slowly to the contrast in temperature from the beach at this time of year. At knee-level depth they faced one another. Ciro's gaze was deep and meaningful as he held both of her hands.

"Really, you do make my heart shake. I want to be with you forever, I want to have a son and I want you to be his mother. My love for you has been tested, it's true ..."

Amalia saw that he was crying, she saw the truth, and she started crying too.

"My love for you is unconditional," he continued. "I would love you even if you ran off with Ote or anyone else. I only want you to be happy, and if that's with someone else someday then I will be happy for you. I don't deserve the joy that you give me."

He reached into his pocket and pulled out a diamond ring. "Will you be my wife, my love, my dear Amalia?"

The diamond shined brightly reflecting the sun—too brightly; it was as though the sun was actually plummeting toward them! It was blinding—he was holding her hands, yes, but he couldn't see her! The bright, blinding sun was hurtling right toward them! His dream had turned into a nightmare as he awoke from the burst of Dr. Neurmer's flash-probe.

"Still normal waves, no hint of a seizure."

Angela stepped out to invite Amalia and Maria back into the room. The doctor ran through a series of commands, paying close attention to the monitor and noting the results.

"Amalia, please tell Ciro your name and ask him to squeeze your hand. Talk to him."

"Ciro, it's Amalia. Can you feel me holding your hand? Squeeze my hand, love. You are doing so much better now. Squeeze my hand, please. Ciro, I need to have you hold my hand again. I need this, please!"

With every ounce of effort he could muster, Ciro tried to move his hand. He assumed she meant his right hand but he sent the mental signal to both, just in case. More than his own pain, he wanted to alleviate hers. He sent the signals but was unsure if the message was received. He knew he was being tested, and his desperation returned as he wondered if he would ever truly wake. He was becoming more and more frantic, struggling to dispel the terrifying thought that he might be awake but unconscious forever!

Chapter 14: It Melts Them Like Ice

Ote and a young German couple were skimming across the mirror-smooth sea to Positano. Here, the restaurants, hotels, and shops employed many of Ote's friends from Praiano. Two of the finest hotels in the world provided work for many of the nearly four thousand people who called Positano home. Much like Praiano, navigating the narrow pedestrian corridors meant either going up or down by foot, the elevation changing with each step. Positano competed with Praiano for the tourists, with each offering a unique experience.

The water taxi from the Grand Spiaggia to Marina di Praia took ten minutes and €30. Ote spent his time at work either taxiing tourists or taking them on coastal day trips. He made €450 per week. His workweek was all seven days from early morning to late evening during the tourist season and he loved his job. He was off from mid-October to the beginning of May. His wife managed a dress shop in town that also catered to tourists. In the summer, Gennaro usually played with his soccer ball, either alone or with the other kids, or hung out at Juliana's mom's house.

Ote had been back at work for five days, and he was spending much of his time at Marina di Praia. With the closing of the Africana, there were fewer tourists staying in Praiano. This trickled down all the way to him. He was on call for when he was needed, but otherwise talked with the employees of the restaurants and bars. After dropping off the Germans, he returned to the marina and resumed the process of patiently waiting.

He was giving Salvatore Pisacane the latest update on Ciro's condition. These updates were provided by Amalia, who phoned him once every morning and once every evening, regardless of any change in condition.

"It's just a matter of time before you two are back fishing the sea and bringing in world-record groupers!" Salvatore said after hearing the latest update.

Ote smiled. That grouper had turned to gold. When coupled with the good news coming from the hospital, he was nearly himself again. He wanted to celebrate with his wife, take her to the attic, and show her his prize. He wanted to liquidate the assets and make them tangible. They deserved it.

But he also knew that if they had found it, someone else had lost it. As happy as he was, someone else was pissed—big-time pissed. He would wait for Ciro to recover, and then together they would decide their next step. For now, he was like a lottery winner who couldn't tell a soul about his windfall.

While his hopes grew, the space in empty boxes in his storage attic shrank. He was now in the habit of telling everyone that sometimes he just needed to get away for a few minutes to the Africana where he and Ciro had spent so much time together. With this excuse planted, he often slipped away to the now-deserted grotto. Each trip brought a backpack-full from the hiding place, gradually relocating the smuggler's illegal imports from the Africana's nooks and crannies to his home.

He would leave his backpack—when full, valued at €1,500,000—unattended at La Praia. It was safe there. Once home, it was even safer. Over the last week he had moved over three hundred packages, each worth €100,000. He did so without any concern that he would be caught.

Ote had decided early in the project that he would move his half first, Ciro's half second. That way Ciro's half would be on top. Accountants call this LIFO, but he didn't refer to it as such. He was exhilarated to truly regain the comfort of his routine.

One week after his return, three weeks after their discovery, and twenty days after Ciro had collapsed, his phone rang. This was his lunchtime. He never went home for lunch before, though now he ate there daily as a convenient way to unload his backpack. It was Amalia, who normally never called at this time. Before Ciro began improving, the sound of the phone would have inspired immediate dread in his chest. Yet now that he was recovering, her unscheduled call could only mean good news—at least that's what he told himself.

He answered *"Ciao,* Amalia!" with more enthusiasm and genuine joy than he had felt in weeks. After listening eagerly for a few moments, he burst out with a *"Fantastico!"* His smile threatened to rip through his ears and sever his brain stem. Tomorrow he would wonder why his face ached, not realizing that he'd strained his smiling muscles.

Ciro had opened his eyes, and reached out, albeit blindly, to Amalia—she was in seventh heaven. Ote could hear Ciro's parents in the background; they too were phoning family and friends with the festive news. Within the hour, all of Praiano's residents would know.

Ote ran to Juliana's dress shop; she jumped into his arms when he gave her the news. He spun her around and around, kissing along the way. It didn't take long for the "Closed for the day" sign to go up in the window.

It was about an hour and a half drive from Praiano to the hospital in Naples during the off-season, but it could take twice that during this congested period of the year. They made it in just less than two hours, traffic having been heavy though surprisingly merciful. This was the first time he would enter the hospital smiling. He and Juliana all but skipped from the parking garage to the entrance. Holding hands, they were as bubbly as just-popped prosecco.

Ciro was propped up in his bed, staring blankly ahead. Amalia ran to Ote and Juliana, hugging Ote first, kissing him over and over, in much the same way a dog would greet its owner after his return from a month-long vacation. She was all but leaping up and down.

"Look at him, doesn't he look great!" Amalia exclaimed.

Ciro really didn't look that great, with his mangy hair and with his frail, pale face mirroring the confusion of a third-grade student in a graduate level physics class at MIT. His parents were at his bedside continuing to stimulate him with affectionate touches and words. They thought he looked great too. Everyone here believed he had never looked better!

Angela had also been summoned, arriving soon after by taxi. She had grown tired of the scornful wow-she-must-be-important looks from the other guests at Il San Pietro and had stopped taking Gio's helicopter. Though deep down she knew the truth was that riding in a helicopter terrified her. She hoped that Ciro's situation would never again become so critical that she would have to endure getting in one again. For some, the drive would have seemed equally as perilous with its ninety-degree blind curves along sheer cliffs that would plunge you directly into the sea. Traveling by water was safest way, but she had no time for that.

As she entered Ciro's room, Angela heard Ludwig Van Beethoven's *Symphony No. 9, Ode to Joy,* the portion near the end of the symphony when the entire chorus bellows undecipherable lyrics, each member seemingly singing from a different song sheet. Much different than the mood presented by Tomaso Albinoni's *Adagio in G Minor* that had filled Angela's ears on all of her previous visits to this room. She translated all of her life experiences into music, and never needed headphones to hear the music that played continuously—it was in her mind, and she heard it in perfect harmony.

"Looks like you all beat me here," she said to the assembled group. "I need to ask everyone to wait outside while I conduct a quick appraisal and review his chart. I promise not to be too long, and I will discuss my findings with you *subito*." Despite many summers in Italy, Angela was shy about her Italian so she was quite proud to have ended on this note.

It was the only part her Italian audience understood. Amalia served as an ad hoc translator when the official translator was absent. Her English was not fluent and she often had to ask Angela to repeat herself more slowly. She was confused by the doctor's use of *subito*, which is how they speak in the north. In the south, they say *presto*.

Angela saw that Ciro was undeniably regaining consciousness. She charted this data and began commanding him to perform tasks, noting her observations in the chart as they went along. Having known Ciro for so many years, she would have liked to join his family and friends in celebrating their joy, but as a doctor she was required to remain professional and view Ciro only as a patient. If a doctor celebrated her great outcomes, logic would insist that they mourn the patients whose outcomes were tragic.

In Ciro's case she made an exception. The data collected was very promising. Angela abandoned her commitment to professional distance, embracing Ciro's family as though it were her own and rejoicing with them in the unexpectedly fortunate turn of events.

She gave Ciro the tempered, encouraging news by means of a hug before departing his room and directing the horde gathered outside his room to a nearby conference closet.

"I want you all to know a few things," she said. "First, Ciro has made a major breakthrough which you yourselves have witnessed. His ability to follow simple commands is very promising, but keep in mind there is still a chance for him to regress back into his unconscious state. Do not be alarmed if this transpires, as it simply happens.

"Second, be aware that upon further waking he will be very confused. Be understanding of his confusion and patient with his recovery. He may not have full command of his arms and legs. He may have to relearn things. He will be a different person, especially in the beginning. I know you all want to go back into the room and celebrate but allow him to rest instead.

I'm only going to allow one person in at a time until I return tomorrow. I know this is difficult but his head is already filled with commotion, we don't want to further that."

Angela stepped toward Ote, her right arm raised for a high-five. He nearly took her hand off with the sound of the clap heard ten meters away at the nurses' station. Angela wryly noted to herself that it was good she was retired—she thought he might have rendered her deft microsurgery hand useless. Smiling as she turned to leave, a disgraceful thought occurred to her, that she could have copped a discrete quick feel had she opted for a hug instead.

The group agreed that Ciro's preferred guest would be Amalia, but each of them would each get five minutes with him every hour or so.

Ote was just a little bit nervous. Angela had spoken of Ciro's confusion but Ote felt confused as well, terrified that Ciro would wake spewing truths and secrets. Was it possible that he would awake and forget that the disk was meant to be their secret? Ote resolved that he would insist that Ciro was talking nonsense, just as the doctor had predicted.

Ciro believed he was in a dream. His senses were dulled, his thinking was even duller. Everything was blurred and latently bright, like the visual effect after the flash of a camera, or rather like after staring directly into a car's headlights from only inches away. He could see the light, but not much else. Sounds were muted as though people were whispering through a wall.

He hadn't retained the conversations between those surrounding him. He couldn't remember his vivid dreams that had flooded and soothed him during his coma. With a flash, indeed with the opening of his eyes, this knowledge evaporated.

Ciro, now truly awake for the first time since his heart attack, was sliding back into sleep. He slept through that day, through the night, and into the next morning. One of his last blurred images was Amalia welcoming Ote into his room.

Without much convincing, Lucio persuaded all but Amalia to stay the night in Gio's penthouse apartment. He was hosting a party, a celebration. He was especially thrilled by the impact Ciro's recovery had had on his wife, Maria, and his daughter, Isabella. Their drained, vacant expressions had been replaced by the vibrancy that had sustained him for so many years. Of course, Lucio also felt the relief of a burden suddenly lifted. Things would soon be again as they had been.

It was a time to celebrate, but Lucio couldn't help thinking about those who wouldn't have the chance to experience this same joy. He had spent more time at the hospital in the last three weeks than he had been in hospitals the rest of his life. He had met new friends who had also been standing vigil for a fallen loved one. He knew that some of them would never experience the joy of a medical miracle like his son's. Those new friends would require lifetimes to heal their wounds, and these thoughts tempered his celebratory mood.

Early the next morning, Ote awoke in Gio's apartment with Juliana by his side. He allowed himself to imagine this type of comfort, the physical comfort that only multitudes of money could ensure, for many years to come. Juliana was still sleeping, and it took all of his strength not to wake her up and tell her what he had found in the disk. His enthusiasm was bubbling over as he kissed her exposed cheek, urging him to buy her all that she had ever desired, everything that she deserved. His son, Gennaro, would have the best, the absolute best of all that his father could find for him. The best soccer camps in Rome ...

These thoughts of spending wildly on his family aroused his senses, and Juliana was awoken by his need. They were curled on their sides facing one another and Ote lightly brushed her bangs across the top of her ear, playing with the strands of her hair, curling them in his fingers as he whispered.

"I am so lucky to have you in my life—you deserve so much more than I have offered you, my dear wife. I just wish I could do more for you and Gennaro."

"Ah, Ote, you provide me with everything that I need. You are all that I need. I know it has been so difficult for you lately, but all is well now."

They quietly made love, for the first time ever on fine, high-thread count sheets, though on this morning they could have made love on the rocky beach with a beach towel for their mattress as they had many times before, and found the same level of comfort that they felt now.

After having showered together, each returning to their same attire from the day before, they made their way into the kitchen where espressos were already being served with light pastries filled with apricot, lemon curd, or chocolate. Maria had already spoken with Angela. Ciro had yet to wake, but Angela said this was real sleep and not to worry.

The doctor had lifted the ban on multiple guests. Today she believed that Ciro would wake with much greater acuity than he had yesterday. She suggested that he would likely be able to talk with those around him and hopefully recognize them.

On the heels of this news, the espressos were gulped in haste; pastries would travel on the road to the hospital. With the sole exception of Amalia's mother's Alfa Romeo, it was a wonder how any of the cars made this trip without breaking down.

Ciro was back in dream, thrilled as he climbed up the three hundred stairs to Amalia's apartment. A blue diamond tinged with a red fire bounced in the front pocket of his tan shorts with each step. It didn't matter to him that his shirt was soaked with sweat. This climb was like baking a cake, adding to it layer by layer. He had withstood more difficult climbs.

It had been years since he'd felt the need to announce his arrival with a knock. He opened the door, but she wasn't sprawled on her black leather sectional as she usually was; she wasn't expecting him. He heard a noise coming from her bedroom down the hall.

The noise excited him as he makes his way to the slightly ajar bedroom door. He had heard these noises before, and quite often. He expected to see her pleasuring herself; he imagined that she was picturing him as she did.

Silently he spied through the slightly open door and then stumbled back. He feared they must have heard him. In this frozen moment he noticed the woodgrain on the door that he'd never paid any attention to in the past. He waited for the door to close on him; instead, the noises became more passionate.

He could hear her encouraging him to go faster. Ciro was shaking like a man dying of hypothermia and wishing he had a gun. He whirled and stormed out and down into the street, nearly knocking over Mrs. Cinque, an elderly widow who was Amalia's neighbor.

Ciro ran down the stairs, futilely fleeing from the images harrowing him. He stumbled on a landing above two hundred feet of stairs and went crashing head over legs, cartwheeling to the bottom. Blood streamed from his ears and mouth. He needed to get to the hospital.

Ciro truly awoke for the first time in twenty-two days. His vision was nearly fully restored and he was thinking clearly, or so he believed. He saw his mother and father first, and he smiles. Then he saw Ote right next to Amalia—the nerve!

Ote expected a smile, but instead he saw Ciro glare at him with a look of pure hatred that burned right through him. For a confused moment he thought it might have something to do with the disk, that he'd stolen its contents or returned it to the police. Ote was completely unprepared, as they all were, for the kind, gentle, Ciro to light up the room with expletives.

"Get the %$@μ out of here before I kill you, you $@!Ω%$@* piece of %$@μ bastard %$@μ!"

He was pointing at Ote. His expression was convulsive, his once-pale face now cardinal red.

The room went still except for Ciro's enraged, jagged breathing. Shock had frozen the smile on Ote's face.

"Ciro, what are you—" Amalia began.

"You no-good whore %&≈†!" Ciro flailed wildly at her, missing her face by a good meter. "Cheap ass tramp hole outrageous lying idiotic cheater! Take your ugly boyfriend out of my room at once and never return, you slut!"

While still frothing at Amalia, Ciro struggled to get out of bed, but his real target was Ote. He was going to kill him. Infuriatingly, his arms and legs weren't quite working yet, and he thrashed impotently.

By now they all thought he was insane, his mind never to be the same again. Ote took his wife's arm, and they hustled out the door. As they took the elevator, Juliana stood calmly next to her husband. She knew through years of experience that Ote would need time to fume, and she was certainly not threatened by Ciro's outrageous accusations.

Ote found himself thinking it would have been easier if Ciro had died. He felt embarrassed and betrayed. After all this time he had spent worrying, praying for Ciro to wake and recover, and this was how he was treated, and in front of so many people he loved?

Lucio cleared the rest of the room, save for his wife. Ciro lunged for Amalia again, and she ran out crying.

She was accustomed to leaving his room in tears—indeed, old habits were difficult to break. Lucio chased after her and took her hand. "Remember what the doctor told us," he said. "It's just confusion." He smiled at her as he seethed inside. The doctor hadn't warned them about anything like this at all.

Lucio returned to his son's room. Maria was sitting beside Ciro, attempting to calm him down. They both felt terrible for Amalia and Ote, but more so they feared that their son had gone mad.

"I am so sorry to have erupted like that," Ciro gasped, "but what you don't know is that before I fell down the stairs near Amalia's apartment, I saw them making love!"

Lucio stifled a smile. "How long do you think you have been in this hospital room?"

"Only one day. Just yesterday I bought her an engagement ring. I couldn't wait to make any clever plan—I had to give it to her right away. And that's when I saw them, in her apartment."

"Ah, my poor dear son, you have had a nightmare. You never fell down any stairs. You have been here over three weeks, unconscious. You had a severe heart attack."

"Lies!"

"Look at this." Lucio unbuttoned Ciro's hospital gown and pointed to the raw incision on his chest. "You see there, that's where they fixed your heart. It was Ote who saved your life. He's spent every minute of the last three weeks here at the hospital with you as you slept. Amalia too. For most of that time, no one believed you would wake."

"That can't be ... I saw them. That wound must be from my fall."

"You have some apologizing to do," Maria snapped. "You attacked the two people that have cared for you the most. Put this silly dream out of your head—it's ridiculous. Here, look at your records."

She pulled his chart from the side of his bed, but Ciro shook his head. He didn't need to see it—in his parents' eyes, he could see the truth. He began to weep weakly.

"What have I done? They will never forgive me—I am better off dead!"

"They'll forgive you, son," said Lucio. "The doctors warned us that you would be confused. Amalia is just outside the door—I'll call her in, and you two can talk. But don't overdo it, you've slept a long time. And if you become confused, tell us! It's to be expected. Just tell Amalia about your nightmare. She'll understand and so will Ote."

They both kissed him, held his hand, and spent the next five minutes reassuring him that a parent's love was true and unchanging.

Amalia was still crying when Lucio gestured for her to join them in the room. His relieved face told her that it was okay. When she saw Ciro, his look told her to run to him. Amalia felt total peace. She lightly placed her hands to his sides and brushed her nose against his, inhaling his love.

His parents slipped out the door to explain to the others, who must have been mortified by their son's behavior. Lucio decided that if would be best if his wife delivered that message and slipped out again, this time down to the parking lot to call Ote and have a smoke.

Ote had made it half way home when his "Hell's Bells" ringtone started screaming. It was Lucio. He had been expecting this call.

With an anomalous diplomacy, Ote told Lucio that he would give Ciro a little more time to heal. After what had been said to him, Ote felt as though he would need time to heal too. Lucio told him that Amalia had forgiven Ciro and that everything now made sense. Lucio did offer that it might be best if Ciro himself explained to Ote why he had lashed out, and assured Ote that he would surely laugh at the explanation.

After just over three weeks without a cigarette, or even the thought of one, Ote pulled into a tobacco store in Sorrento to buy a pack. Even now he didn't realize that he hadn't missed them; he didn't even realize he had quit. He only knew that it was time for a ciggybaba.

His first three ciggybabas tasted terrible to him after not having had one in so long, but he got through this distaste just about when he made it back to Praiano.

Chapter 15: Now Thru the Game

Ote hadn't slept well the night before. He hadn't been able to get Ciro's brutal accusations out of his mind, nor could he stop obsessing over the stash in his attic. As the two thoughts were emotionally contradictory, they continually tugged at the other, making for tossing and turning all night long. For Ote who seldom experienced equilibrium even on his best days, this was just another sleepless night. This was not to say that he was unhappy in life—quite the opposite in fact; he was very happy despite his propensity to let what others said influence his poise.

Ote sat slumped at the small rectangular wooden dining table for four, occasionally flashing a not-so-convincing smile. He barely tasted the French toast that Juliana had made for him. As loving as she was, Juliana had never been his confidant—a burden he didn't wish to bestow upon her, especially at this moment. It was a very demanding position that Ciro, and no one else, had managed well for his entire life.

Forgiveness would be tough for Ote, and at this moment he had no intention of hearing Ciro's excuse for his behavior. He wasn't going to be taken in so easily like Amalia and the rest. His crushed ego required time to mend and for once he wouldn't have Ciro to lean on while he mended.

He could have forgiven the words, in and of themselves, on almost any other occasion but after what he had been through and his expectations of how a loving, appreciative Ciro would welcome him as a hero, as the man who saved his life—well, this struck deep within his spirit. Yesterday after returning to the La Praia, he had to endure the continuous barrage of "We heard Ciro is doing so much better—you must be thrilled!" from everyone he passed. Far from thrilling, every mention of Ciro ground salt into his lacerated mind.

Today was likely to be worse than yesterday, as the American doctor and her husband had reserved a day trip beginning at the lunch hour. He liked Angela and her husband, but he just couldn't picture a day at sea with them talking constantly of Ciro this and Ciro that. He thought he just might vomit all over them. He even considered quitting his job—he didn't have to work any more—he had his attic stash and as far as he was concerned it was *all* his now.

He would have no problem telling Ciro (whenever he might speak with him again) that the disk had disappeared sometime during his three-week stay at the hospital. Ote already believed that Ciro had only backed off his threat to kill him because he had suddenly remembered the disk. *Sorry about your luck*, Ote thought. Whether this thought was motivated by revenge or greed, it suited Ote just the same. He rarely defined things. He rarely felt the need.

Meanwhile, Angela strode into Ciro's room and was not surprised to see Amalia, Lucio, and Maria seated next to him.

"Hi, Dr. Angela," Ciro said in a bright voice. "They tell me I should have been calling you *Dr.* Angela all this time, seeing how you're the only person in the world who could have saved my life. I'm sorry that I never treated you with the reverence one should accord such a woman!"

Angela smiled. This interaction could have ended her examination right then. She was pleased that his cognitive skills were so sharp so soon.

"I was taken aback by your lack of respect on more than one occasion," she said with a smirk, "but I gave you a pass as I didn't figure a person of your background could know better."

Ciro grinned right back. "I seem to remember that you had many professions over the years. Let's see—you were a chief financial officer for some large company, a trust-fund baby who never worked, and an oilrig manager who had given herself to the perilous northern seas. I figured you couldn't hold a job!"

This room filled with laughter.

This was all translated back and forth by Amalia. When the translator arrived a few minutes later, Angela asked her to transcribe her notes into Italian for the chart. She was enjoying Amalia's translated exchange.

When Angela went over to Ciro to perform a series of pokes and prods, he reached out and grabbed her, pulling her in for what he must have believed was a big bear hug; Angela genuinely hugged him back, being sure not to snap this now-dainty flower of a man, enervated from weeks of laying in a hospital bed, and noted his lack of strength in the charts.

"Thank you so much Dr. Angela," Ciro said with tears in his eyes. "Really, I had no idea."

"We're all pleased that you have returned from the unknown," Angela replied meaningfully.

Following a five-minute question-and-answer period with the patient and family—with the official translator interpreting as she always did when it was an official doctor-patient exchange—Angela asked the woman to return to her note transcription and let Amalia resume her translation.

"I did have to hire a new boat captain though," said Angela. "Ote's taking us out this afternoon. What a friend you have in him—it's my understanding that he never left your side, and he's the one that you should thank for saving your life. Without his quick actions, you would never have gotten to the hospital in time. With your permission, I will give him the good news of your progress, though I'm sure he already knows."

Ciro's parents and Amalia shifted uncomfortably.

"Didn't anyone write into my charts what an ass I made of myself yesterday?" Ciro asked. "I'm surprised that Amalia is even here. I have never been so angry and hateful; I struck out at those who love me most. Ote refused my call last night and I don't blame him. I woke up thinking I'd been in the hospital only for a day and acted upon a nightmare that I had. I'll speak with him when I get out of course, but I'm not sure that I can express to him what I need to express over the phone."

"He'll forgive you, and please don't feel guilty about it," said Angela. "I see this all the time. Your brain is still healing— give it some time and you'll be back at it. You know what I've learned most in my time here? The Italian mentality of 'Why not start now?' That, and your love of home, family, and friends. Everyone is so proud of their community—you stand together, and everyone treats the other like family, which means so much here. I don't have a friend like Ote and I have many friends that I have known since forever. In America old friends usually drift apart—there's no community fabric that holds the family and friendships together like there is here."

Angela smiled again. "But now for the bad news—did I mention that my husband and I are buying a place here? You will have to stop treating us like tourists now; we'll be residents. *And* now you must treat me with the proper respect owed to the *great* doctor that I am!"

They all agreed this was wonderful news. They tripped over themselves suggesting villas for sale that would be just perfect for her, all in Praiano.

Before she left the hospital, Angela changed Ciro's therapy orders to physical therapy twice daily and speech therapy daily. She told Lucio, privately, that Ciro would probably be discharged in a week's time, but tempered that optimistic prognosis with the admonition that it would only happen if everything continued along this current path. She had consulted with Ciro's heart surgeon, who explained that the three weeks he was in the coma had actually benefited his heart, so there was no risk that his heart would delay his discharge.

On Angela's return trip to Positano she answered a call from Gio, who was thrilled to learn that Ciro might be home in a week.

"You must be just as happy as his family," said Gio, "and you deserve that happiness. It must feel wonderful to see how your skills have brought so much joy."

"Ciro's will to live won out—I just nudged his will along a bit, that's all. But yes, in this case—my last case—it was incredibly gratifying to witness the progression from crushed to jubilant hearts. And having known Ciro for years, it was all the more momentous, and surprisingly personal. It's nice to be human and share in the joy for once. It's a great way to end a career."

"I read about how you Americans retire. In any case we have our agreement to conclude, contingent of course on the absence of setbacks in your last patient's recovery. Call me early next week and I'll make arrangements for you and your husband to view the villas. It will be a tough choice! I often can't decide where to stay myself. And just so there's no confusion, our agreement states that a villa will be available to you for as long as you like, but I'll retain ownership. This is good for you—it's like owning it without incurring the expenses of owning it, if you know what I mean."

"Yes, that's my understanding as well. Todd and I find your gift very generous and appreciate your consideration. No problems there. We are actually going to take the boat today to see them from the sea—we have a favorite chosen from the road's view, but we want to be very thorough. I'll let you know if there's a change in Ciro's condition, and we will look forward to seeing you next week."

"Very good, Dr. Neurmer, and again thank you for interrupting your vacation to help out a local. I'm sure everyone is very appreciative of your fine efforts, no one more than me!"

Angela couldn't quite put a finger on what it was precisely, but Gio seemed to be taking a great deal of interest in—and spending a great deal of money on—someone he didn't know. It was very strange, but she figured it was a cultural misunderstanding on her part. She was looking forward to spending more time here so that she would have a greater appreciation for what made these people tick.

"Well, Ote, you are looking much better than when I last saw you!" Angela said when she greeted him on the dock. Had she stopped there, perhaps all would have been well. "You must have patched things up with Ciro!"

Ote's rage deepened. Who told this American about what had passed between him and Ciro? He gave her a tight smile. "They tell me he was confused. I'm just glad he's better."

This was more than true a couple days back, but now, even Ote wasn't sure. No doubt Ote had recently been put through the wringer, from the lowest of lows to the highest of highs only to be slammed back down.

Angela's blunder would set the tone for Ote the rest of the day. He was certain—and this realization began to obsess him—that Ciro had told Angela about his blowup and asked her to make things right. That's why they wanted him to take them along the coast. But Ote was too smart to fall for that. He would feed Angela and Todd faulty information the entire boat ride, which she would then report back to Ciro. *I'm a veritable genius*, Ote thought as he considered his countermeasures.

Several miles down the coast, Ote pulled alongside the cliffs, so the Neurmers could inspect *Gio le Ville*, as they were known. He only caught part of the English conversation, mostly spoken too fast with many phrases unknown to him. He was not bad at English, but only when it came at a methodical pace devoid of idioms.

He saw their smiles as they pointed to each of the villas, so he knew they made them happy but learned little else. "Which one would you choose?" Todd asked him.

"I no like any of them," Ote responded in his most despondent voice.

What's there to like in seaside mansions, each worth millions of Euro, for a guy living in a slightly run-down five-room apartment? Ote was pleased with his response—he needed to make them think he was major-league bummed, even though he had forgiven Ciro. If merchandise worth millions upon millions of Euro had been stolen from him, he would be bummed, so he played bummed.

"*None* of them?" Todd persisted. "How could you not like any of them?"

Gio gave *them a villa?* "My English not so good today. Bad day—I happy that Ciro better but something else." Ote thought he should be an actor; he was so good at this.

It was easy for Ote from this point on. Quiet and quieter when it came to verbal interaction, he had convinced himself, especially after he noticed them whispering, that the Neurmers were talking about him and probably discussing how best to manipulate him.

Ote kept up his despondent character for the next four days, even around his wife. He only let his guard slip with Gennaro, his new fishing partner. Ote took great measures to move his boat away from others boats so he could let out his genuine ultra-happy self with his son. If he hadn't let himself rejoice, he thought he would implode.

On the fifth day of his performance that, incidentally, was more reminiscent of a porn star's than Academy Award–winner's, he decided it was time to check in with Ciro. By this point he had made it widely known to all that his depressed state had nothing to do with Ciro. It was something else entirely, something that he couldn't talk about. To those who knew about the blowup, he maintained that he had forgiven Ciro and that he knew all about the dream and the blameless confusion that it had caused. Yet if everything Ote claimed to believe were true, he would have called his friend. But he hadn't, not yet. He would only do so now to further his plan.

Ciro answered the phone and heard the voice of his

oldest friend. "Sorry I haven't been back to see you, Ciro, but I've been hiding from the assassins you hired to kill me!"

Ote found this ingenious. It had come right to him, unrehearsed.

"Ote, I wanted to see you in person. I'm so sorry, but I was not myself. I want to see you as soon as I get out, maybe even tomorrow. They tell me that I might get out tomorrow. Oh, I'm so glad you called—I've been lying here worrying, thinking that you hated me!"

"I have some bad news, Ciro. Are you alone?"

"Yes, all by myself."

"Everything's gone, Ciro—the disk, everything. Someone took it while I was with you at the hospital—it's all gone!"

"I don't understand what you are saying. What is gone? What disk?"

Ote hadn't prepared for this response, though he should have, given that Ciro had just woken from a brain injury. He removed the phone from his ear and tried to think.

"Ah, Ote, you're playing a trick on me! Trying to get even. I don't blame you, I feel horrible for what I said."

"I was just testing your mind, making sure you were really better!"

They talked just as they had before the heart attack. Ciro wanted to know everything that had happened that night. When Ote realized that Ciro had no memory of that night, he had a tough time not jumping through the roof. It was still possible that Ciro was playing a trick of his own. If he was pretending to forget, then they were both very convincing with their lies.

Ote explained that Ciro had become ill after they caught the grouper, violently ill, and that he had taken the boat to the Africana, thinking it was a stomach issue. Ote then used the truth to guide the shaping of his lies, ending with him crashing ashore.

Ciro laughed at the story. Ote kept waiting for Ciro to say

"Ah, ha! You weren't going to tell me about the disk if I pretended to forget, were you?" but Ciro never did.

Ote hung up unsure about many things. Maybe Ciro had truly forgotten, maybe he hadn't been conspiring against him all along, and finally maybe it just didn't matter. To be sure and definitively allay his fears, Ote decided that he would continue to act miserable. And if Ciro really had forgotten, well then, it must be Ote's lucky day!

In the past, Ote had always been generous, taking from what little he had to give to others. Now that he had so much to give, greed was overwhelming his character.

In the past, if either had been so consumed in their own thoughts, the other would have noted that and repaired the problem. Now they were both captives of their own minds and their demons that were increasingly poisoning them.

Before his heart attack, Ciro had vowed every morning to live this day as though it were his last. He had lived without fear of death, forgiven himself and others, and although he didn't know it, his appreciation of his everyday fantastic life distinguished him from almost everyone.

But since his return from the hospital, every day was filled with dread that he might drop again at any second. This caused a great deal of depression, which he mostly hid behind a mask of forced joy. Ote would have seen through the mask had he himself not been tortured by his own angst.

In the week Ciro had been home, Ote played his role of great friend to the hilt. They moved back into their routine except for one detail—they hadn't really discussed anything at all. It was a different, defiantly yet quietly self-absorbed friendship where conversations were object-oriented with no subjective thoughts shared or solicited.

Ote mistook Ciro's depression as being related to the disk. He endlessly tried to determine whether Ciro knew and yet said nothing. This motivated Ote to spend time with someone he now perceived as an enemy.

This baseless, contorted notion struck Ote as a profound insight. Since the onset of his good fortune, he had tended to be more inquisitive than he'd been before. And more clever, as he continued to portray a downtrodden ghost of himself, with shoulders slumped but still communicating a contrived "There's nothing wrong with me!" exuberance. It was a very complicated role, being a tormented yet uncomplaining soul.

His contempt for Ciro had ripened. Forty years of fabulous experiences together had been relabeled as wasted time. Two minutes' worth of Ciro's scathing words—now conveniently fueling his greed—spoiled four decades of remarkable memories filled with laughs, smiles, and adventure. And just like that, good riddance.

Since the homecoming Ote had been in constant battle with himself. At times he saw the real Ciro he had known forever and at other times he saw the conniving Ciro who wanted to trick him out of his treasure. And Ote was obviously not acting like Ote, but Ciro was too depressed—and too busy pretending not to be—to see it.

Chapter 16: You Are Changeable

Alessio's last day in London would prove to be his finest. His quick business trip away from Aprajita and their son had only served to reinforce his love for them both.

It was 79 degrees, a sunny London Monday. Alessio felt both inspired and amazed by his good fortune. He kept gazing up to the heavens, now blocked by a cloudless blue sky, and praising the day. As they walked through the streets he kept glancing over at his son and Aprajita—he had missed her shine during these two years he'd spent thinking of her.

They lunched at the Dell Restaurant, seated beneath a framed black-and-white poster advertising a free concert from the summer of 1969 by the band Blind Faith—Eric Clapton, Steve Winwood, Ginger Baker, and Rick Grech.

Alessio knew that his faith wasn't blind—his blessings were very vivid, very real, and surrounding him at that very moment. He couldn't get over the fact that here sat his son. Ramesh had a full head of jet-black curls, bright blue eyes, and a giggly smile. His carefree attitude inspired his father's faith.

Alessio had already pictured himself rallying with Ramesh on the tennis court and kicking a soccer ball in the backyard. It was never too early to start, not even in the waddling toddler stage, so Alessio believed. He rested his head on Ramesh's neck and savored his fresh infant scent. Alessio saw, smelled, tasted, felt, and heard his faith through his son who in just a few days had brought him closer to his Lord.

After lunch, they made the quick walk to a grassy area in Hyde Park known as the Dell. They plopped down between the Queen Caroline Memorial and the Holocaust Memorial near a small gurgling stream—the aptly named twisting Serpentine. They both kept a close eye on Ramesh as he frolicked, mostly running in circles around them, falling more than occasionally and laughing all the way to the ground.

"Duck!" Ramesh said in English, pointing toward the bank of the Serpentine while mimicking the duck's walk as he attempted to get a closer look.

"Mama! Duck!"

"Mama! Mama! Duck!"

"PAPA! Duck!"

Alessio did not even try to hide the impact of hearing his son calling him "Papa" for the first time. Aprajita heard it too; she looked up at Alessio to see his beaming smile as tears flowed steadily down his cheeks. She put her arm around him and cradled her head onto his while they both enjoyed this precious view of their son at play. They laughed and held each other tighter, watching Ramesh the duck race after the Serpentine duck.

"Do you know how much I love him?" Alessio asked. "In less than one day he has brought me more happiness than I've enjoyed in lifetime. Look at his joy, still innocent."

He turned toward Aprajita and lightly brushed the nape of her neck. "This joy you have given me—I know now why I thought of you often. I love you so dearly. I don't wish to frighten you by saying this, but it's true."

"Sweet Alessio, who couldn't love you?" Aprajita asked, snuggling closer to him. "I couldn't even dream of such a day as today. It's a miracle, our chance encounter."

Their fond embrace ended with a soft kiss as they looked deeply into the eyes of each other, the loving intensity in their eyes confirming their words.

Chapter 17: Well-Being Is Vain and Always Fades to Nothing

"Stunning, they are all stunning! One last question—will they retain the exterior color over time or might they be painted a different color in the future?"

"The stucco contains the color, Dr. Neurmer. The color will fade over time but I'm required to maintain the colors as they are."

"They were nearly identical, but we've finally chosen this wonderful home—the Villa Calypso!"

Todd, Angel and Gio were sitting in wrought-iron chairs with richly padded eggshell-colored cushions. The fifty-square-foot rectangular wrought-iron table boasted a brightly glazed ceramic tabletop with azure blues and canary yellows depicting a nautical compass.

They were in what Gio called the "shade nook" wing of the terrace that was set off the main terrace near the wading pool and surrounded by three walls of sculpted evergreens reaching twenty feet in height. Todd was systematically scanning everything, absorbing all he dared.

The terrace was two-tiered. They were seated on the lower, larger tier atop sharp gray limestone paving stones of various sizes arranged in a ninety-degree pattern. The upper-level terrace of cream marble was reached by three arched eight-meter-wide steps hewn from the same marble.

"My favorite from the beginning," Todd confirmed. He had left the decision entirely up to his wife. So far as he was concerned, they could have picked one of the villas from a hat. This felt like one of those great acts of God that he had read about in the newspaper, or more likely, online.

"Villa Calypso it is!" Gio said with a wry smile. "This was

my favorite too!" he said, and frowned. "Oh well, that's what I get for offering. I was hoping to dissuade you by keeping the staff from cleaning this one over the last weeks!"

To Todd the villa was spotless. It suddenly occurred to him that he'd have to spend half of every day cleaning the place.

Gio smiled at Todd's sudden look of consternation. "I've asked the maid to be out of here within the hour so you might have the villa to yourselves—but don't worry, Mr. Neurmer, she'll be back every four days to do your bidding!"

They all laughed, the Neurmers more than Gio. After a few more instructions, Gio left them the keys.

"Oh, I wanted to invite you aboard the boat sometime next week for a small party with Ciro and his family and friends. It will be a pleasure to finally meet them. Father Viglianti is arranging it. Can I confirm you pending a firm date?"

"How wonderful!" Angela said, once again answering for both of them. "Of course we'll be there, with or without notice. Thank you so much." This began a flurry of thank yous from both Todd and Angela.

Right after Gio left, rather drunk with their thank yous, Todd could see Angela twirling the villa's keys as she danced a ballet around the terrace. He went to his backpack and pulled out his iPod. His dance had already begun even as he ported his iPod into the stereo and turned the volume up to jet-engine loud, so that the beginning of Grieg's "In the Hall of the Mountain King," usually whispery, was thunderous. The cellos and bassoons kicked off the piece slowly, but the French horns and bass, along with the entire orchestra, would soon enough join in the effort to carry this piece along slowly but surely.

With the bass, Todd started in almost slow motion, tiptoeing *sempre* staccato in rhythm with his knees together, lifting high one at a time as though he were theatrically sneaking up on someone. Indeed, he was stalking his wife

Angela, who was laughing at him while she kept to her preferred dance partner, the villa's keys.

When the bassoon extended the *buoooo*, Todd attempted to maintain his balance, freezing in midair with one knee up, but he lost his balance before the strings took over in a repetitive melody. As the pace quickened with the addition of the finger-plucking violins, piccolos, and clarinets, so did Todd with his legs, which blurred like the pistons of an engine. Then the entire orchestra was in chaos as were his steps, which finally convinced Angela to give him a vulnerable look and join him in dance.

Now both circled as Angela tried to catch up with the music and Todd tried to catch his breath when the troll-courtiers, the imp, the maiden, the witch with the ladle, and the witch with butcher knife erupted into accusations of treacherous acts and threats of subsequent punishment in beautifully unrecognizable lyrics sung with bile toward the guilty: "Slay him! The Christian's son has bewitched the Mountain King's fairest daughter! *Slagt ham! Slagt ham!*"

Well, if it must be so, Edvard Grieg.

It was time to rock this villa when the chorus of troll-courtiers' frenzied voices of condemnation made it impossible for Todd and Angela to keep up with the tornadic pace. "Ice to your blood, friends!" sang Todd the Mountain King as he grabbed Angela, singing with the ultimate decree to the accused who, not so wisely, had done this bewitching thing with the *fairest* daughter of the King, though it would have been equally unwise to do any bewitching thing with any of the King's daughters, fairest or not.

Whatever to this Mountain King mumbo jumbo, Todd thought, *it's time to get back to dancing*, and in ballroom style they bounded and leaped across the marble, spinning her and himself round and round as the music commanded their bodies to thrash-dance in circles until they both lay dizzy and laughing on the marble floor.

Todd was coughing-laughing, his chest heaving heavily into hers. He exercised daily and was in great shape, but he had never danced like that before. They lay there, holding hands, smiling, and digging for breath.

"Let's play a game of hide and seek!" Angela wasn't a good asker. "I'll count to sixty from outside on the terrace, and I promise not to look!"

"I can tell you where you'd be wasting your time looking—anywhere but the bedrooms!" Todd said with a blazing smile, looking up at her as she leaned over him and stared back.

Todd ran up the stairs as loudly as he could, then quickly opened and shut doors even louder before sneaking back down the stairs and hiding with seconds to spare behind the armoire near the double doors opening onto the terrace. Angela was again dancing to "In the Hall of the Mountain King" as she tiptoed up the stairs, ignoring the new song that played in the background.

Once she was past the landing, Todd snuck outside to the deck. He sauntered toward the pool, casually disrobing along the way to mark his trail. Angela saw the whole naughty display from her view out the landing's window that overlooked the terrace.

She ran quickly back down the stairs, entered the temperature-controlled wine closet, and then popped back out with a bottle of champagne. And to the china cabinet where she grabbed two champagne glasses, filling them and moving back out the terrace doors in less than a minute as Prokofiev's "Dance of Knights" heralded her entry. She took long, parading strides, perfectly stamping each foot to the beat of the basses, kettledrums, and baritones. *Bom! Bwam! Bom!*

When the violins, French horns, and the rest enrolled in the clamor with increasing pace, so did Angela. There would be time to softly pirouette later—for now she marched, gathering her breath.

Then she pranced serpentine, back and across, using the entire terrace as her dance floor as she gradually advanced toward the pool. With a *petit saut* she landed in front of him. In yet another demonstration of her deft hands, not a drop of champagne spilled.

"You cheated!" he protested.

She raised her glass and proceeded to toast:

"To my loveliest husband, who like a precious bottle of Bordeaux has improved with age and is now more delicate, savory, and desired by me beyond what I dared to believe was possible. I know you have tolerated my impatience and occasional rudeness. I really did try to keep my work outside our home, but it was so difficult to turn off. I could never escape the faces of those so desperate for my help. But now it's truly behind us, and I intend to make it up to you every chance I get. *Salute*, my only!"

Todd raised his glass high. "Off with your clothes and join me, my newly obedient wife!"

He stared intently as she obeyed his command—he liked that, and he wondered what type of erotic fantasy she would choose to play out this time. He considered the possible options as Angela sat with her legs slightly apart at the pool's edge and waved him in with her foot.

They had almost finished their first glass of champagne, and probably would have made it through the first glass into the second, when Ravel's "Jeux d'eau" came on. So they grasped joy in the water too, through several more songs, only seeing the beautiful vistas as reflected by their passionate lover's eyes. The whoosh of the sea roared into the crags below them in time with their lovemaking.

Angela's philosophy on taking advantage of the house while the servants were gone spelled for much more of the same for the next few days, with a hike into the village sprinkled in for fresh tomatoes, basil, lemons, oregano, garlic, eggs, prosciutto, breads, fish, clams, figs, olives, almonds, zucchini, buffalo mozzarella, pasta paired with two cases of locally bottled whites and reds, ten cases of water, tea bags for iced tea, coffee, and chocolate-filled croissants. When Todd saw how much his wife had bought, he was pleased to learn that the store delivered.

The delivery kid was the last one to see or speak to them for five entire days until Gio's assistant phoned Angela to confirm the pending dinner cruise aboard the *Thetis*. There would be a theme to the gathering, "Heaven on Earth," and Gio had outfits for the evening delivered to the Neurmers that morning that were again, somehow, a perfect fit. The costumes were white designer cloth of silk and linen that draped head-to-toe with matching handmade white leather sandals.

They floated down the steps to the dock that served all four villas, raptly speculating about the night to come. Today, said Angela, would be the first time in her career that she celebrated a recovery with her patient, and she thought it would be quite satisfying to finally stop denying herself this personal indulgence.

They glided across the sea with the wind in their faces aboard the *Thetis's* tender, a twin outboard fiberglass raft that seated six.

On the lower deck cheering their arrival were Gio, Ciro, Father Viglianti, Ciro's parents, Ote, Juliana, Gio's girlfriend, and Amalia. They were all dressed in white but each outfit was unique and suited to the wearer's personal style.

As they prepared to pull alongside the yacht, Angela wondered yet again why Gio was so thrilled, and why he had paid for all of this despite having seemingly no stake in any of it.

But not everyone has ulterior motives and those who do, certainly don't always harbor dastardly ones. Gio's motive was the rush he found in surprising others with his particular brand of joy. Apparently Angela, a direct beneficiary of Gio's astonishing generosity, must have missed that fact.

For years Gio had randomly mixed into the crowds along the coast in search of younger tourists to invite aboard his yacht for a couple days so he could share in their lives and create a meaningful experience filled with whatever his guests might desire.

Gio could and did provide whatever they desired, from the legal to the proscribed. Although he personally only indulged in the legal, he made no distinction between, say, sugar, a naturally growing plant that's highly addictive and a leading cause of obesity, diabetes, cardiovascular disease, and a host of quack ADD medications and, say, cocaine, which has a nearly identical chemical makeup and is similarly addictive and caustic to one's health. He noted that society just chose not to load children up on the cocaine variety.

For two days the lucky couples cruised the coast, jet-skied, snorkeled around the Gali Islands, dined, and danced, and Gio played the perfect host. He had been doing this for years, usually choosing his guests by getting to know random people he selected while out dining out with his girlfriend.

Just joining him at a previous dinner wasn't enough to win access aboard; he needed to get a feel for their demeanor first. Gio had three photo albums filled with the smiling faces of the winners with their names and contact information and a handwritten paragraph or two offering Gio's insight into the couple.

Gio had never lost his curiosity in others' lives; lives told a story. Each life was unique, and when unearthed properly he could rid them of the contamination of their contradictory beliefs that had always been instilled by others since the beginnings of their lives.

Gio liked nothing more than entering people's lives and stopping their monstrous spinning wheel on "Live two days like the wealthiest person on the planet." Gio hated that spinning wheel—he avoided it in his life, but he also knew most others allowed the wheel to spin every day. Even at dinner, the wheel might turn up. "Sorry, the chef is in a foul mood because his wife left him and he really doesn't care about how your food tastes." Why allow a bad meal or any other uncontrollable thing to affect one's thoughts, which in turn affected one's way?

If Gio knew what Angela was thinking, he would suggest she read Pyrrho, an ancient philosopher who believed that all things are essentially indistinguishable, immeasurable, unable to be decided, and no more this than that, or both this and that and neither this nor that. Pyrrho concluded that human senses neither transmitted truths nor lied. Humanity could not know the inner substance of things, only how things appeared. Gio often wondered why people wondered. Gio was a person who *lived* each day to the fullest, without regret, without worry about yesterday nor tomorrow, and he had no expectations in anything other than himself—and he expected very little of himself.

He learned of another ancient philosopher, Epicurus, while at college in America. Epicurus gave him comfort in the concept of ataraxia, which carried him through a severe depression filled with dumbfounded disbelief. Ataraxia was a way of life for him now. When one was aboard Gio's boat the theme of every party was "Heaven on Earth" and it was his intent to allow people to escape their thoughts and truly experience the now with no promise of anything in the future.

After a forty-minute cruise along the Amalfi coast where the guests mingled, mostly discussing how good things looked—the other guests, the coastline, the yacht, the weather, and the cocktails. They missed the smells, the sounds, the touches, and the tastes as they focused on how things looked, which oftentimes is not important at all. Some people look good until they drop dead.

As the yacht set anchor, everyone assembled on the second deck, still in white and holding their favorite drink. Most were looking at the island of Capri—at this time of day it appeared as if the Faraglioni that rip through the clear blue sea are rockets gathering themselves for liftoff as the sun sparkling on the sea around them looked like rocket flames.

"I'd like to put on a CD of Carl Orff," said Gio, "who, nearly one hundred years ago, wrote the musical scores to an ancient manuscript over a thousand years old—*Carmina Burana.* Specifically 'O Fortuna,' a piece that we have all heard numerous times though I doubt if many of you know the lyrics and the story they tell of the monstrous spinning wheel of fate.

"Take Ciro. For so many years the wheel was kind to him. And then one day, and without warning, the wheel turns up a tragedy that he barely survives. But as it's always spinning—in some people's minds—it finally brings us here together to celebrate another day of heaven on earth. Look around you— hear the sounds, smell, taste, savor the incredible views, and feel their impact. In front of you is card with that ancient poem translated into both Italian and English."

And with his remote control he cued up "O Fortuna" and upon the first note everyone realized they had in fact had heard the piece many times in commercials and movies. Certainly neither Ote nor Ciro noted that the moon had gone from motionless to ever-changing, nor had Todd Neurmer.

O Fortuna, velut luna, statu variablilis
semper crescis aut decrescis
vita detestabiles
nunc obdurate et tunc curat ludo menis aciem
egestatem, potestatem, dissolvit ut glacium
Sors immanis et inanis, rota tu volubilis
Status malus, vana salus, semper dissolubilis
Obumbrata et velata michi quoque niteris
Nunc per ludum dorsum nudum fero tui sceleris
Sors salutis et virtuties michi nunc contraria
Est affectus et defectus semper in angaria
Hac in hora sine mora corde pulsum tangite
Sortem sternit fortem,

Mecum omnes plangite!

"Oh Fortune, like the moon you are changeable, ever waxing and waning; hateful life first oppresses then soothes as fancy takes it; power and poverty, it melts them like ice.

"Fate—monstrous and empty, you whirling wheel, you are malevolent, well-being is vain and always fades to nothing, shadowed and veiled, you plagued me too. Now through the game I bring my bare back to your villainy.

"Fate is against me in health and virtue, driven on and weighted down, always enslaved. So at this hour without delay pluck the vibrating strings; since fate strikes down the strong man; everyone weep with me!"

After "O Fortuna" ended, Gio stood up again. "If only for this evening vacate your mind of the thoughts that might disrupt this very moment—and the next and the next and the next. Abandon anything preconceived about what this night should bring and bask in the moment instead. No one knows what tomorrow will bring, so don't dwell upon convictions of others from the past that masquerade as what you believe you know."

Gio began all of his dinner gatherings for his first-time guests in this very same way. Father Viglianti was the only guest present who had seen it before. Like Gio, he was a true believer and had been ever since he first met Gio some seven years earlier. Viglianti really hadn't liked him much back then—he found Gio's fingers to be dirty and smeared with evil.

Ote was the first to take advantage of Gio's offer.

"Can I plug my iPod into your stereo? I have the same song, though a little bit less classical, more of a dance version. And I propose we dance!"

Ciro was still absorbed by the lyrics printed on his card when Amalia grabbed him and led him toward the outer terrace. Gio's girlfriend grabbed Father Viglianti, Todd grabbed Angela, and Lucio grabbed Maria.

Ote's version was a classic bass-thumping techno sub beat surrounding an otherwise clean "O Fortuna." It began identically to the one they had just heard, but then it blew out with the bass-thumping, drums popping, and symbols splashing.

They danced in a ballet of irregular, convulsive movements. Lucio and Maria, not really that much older than the rest and still enflamed by the miraculous recovery of their son, stepped it up with a high-energy, valley-free, swing style dance.

Todd marched in place as he air-drummed a set of kettles, accentuating it all with a stern torso that, despite the flogging of his arms and the trooping of his legs, remained motionless. Angela danced behind him like a jack-in-the-box, bending fluidly with her knees to the thump of the bass, shimmering with the symbols down low, then popping back up again while somehow managing to avoid his flaring limbs—as a pair, they were quite impressive.

Beside them, also trying to avoid Todd, but less successfully than Angela, were Ote and Juliana on one side and Ciro and Amalia on the other. Their dancing was no holds barred—you needed to give them extra space or they'd knock you to the ground.

For the moment, the group had returned to their groove. Juliana and Amalia tempted each other while Ote and Ciro banged shoulders until Ote nearly toppled over his erstwhile friend. Ciro was risking himself in his euphoria, but he had forgotten that he was depressed and his rag-doll whipping gyrations threatened to tear him apart at the seams.

With surprising skill, Father Viglianti made the role of axis seem simple as Gio's girlfriend wheeled around the priest with her right index finger extended toward his forehead.

Gio was one of the better dancers, in rhythm to the constant jackhammering bass drum.

Though clad in all white, they hardly resembled angels;

they were more like a blizzard of wind-whipped snow.

Their dancing established the tone for the entire evening—even the Americans seemed to be totally focused on the bombardment of stimuli. There would be no drab gossip about someone else, or somewhere else. No, this party's wheel was landing on diamonds, pearls, gold, and sapphires.

During dinner, airy futuristic sounds of a new age played softly in the background, coaxing the conversation toward the nature of one's fate. They debated the meaning of the spinning wheel of fortune, the personality of the man who had penned the poem, and what his world was like when he wrote it. Their questions were largely addressed to Gio, and he contributed nuances of detail that the others would most likely not have managed. He cited other poems and songs from the *Carmina Burana* collection to reinforce his position when challenged— usually by the soft-spoken pair of Ote and Ciro.

Gio was highly versed in many aspects of ancient times and painted a very holistic picture without offending the faithful Catholics present. He certainly didn't sermonize—he just presented his facts in great detail and never once made arguments based on faith.

By now the sun had slipped away, and a layer of clouds blanketed the horizon in shades of purple, gray, and black. At the peak of Capri a glistening-gold, burnt-tangerine sky reached for the heavens. The ever so slight rocking of the yacht was hypnotically combined with the food, wine, view, astral background music, and Gio's history lesson.

As they set into their fourth course of food and wine, Ciro sat dying for a cigarette. He hadn't had one in nearly a month and missed them dearly. It was especially difficult when others smoked in front of him. And it didn't help that he was drunk—Ciro's doctor had recommended that he drink deep dry reds, and Ciro had readily obliged.

Just as the main course, filet of veal, was presented, Todd suddenly wobbled to his feet. "Oh my," he said rapidly. "I forgot to phone my daughter. If you'll excuse me, I won't be long. Of course please don't wait on me."

Todd felt that what he needed was some fresh air, except they were dining in open air already. He moved to the rear of the boat cautiously, as if seasick, holding onto whatever ledge was available with each step. This rather odd retreat did not go unnoticed by anyone, and certainly not by Angela, who bolted from her chair and ran after him.

She put her arm around him and he reciprocated with his arm around her. They made it over to a couch, where he plummeted in a heap. His forehead was aglow with perspiration; his hair around the edges was soaked. His skin was pale as ash and his wide eyes told the story: as if paralyzed, he watched as the wheel with a last click rotated past "Food Poisoning" and landed on "Impending Doom." Who knows— perhaps with another click the wheel would have landed on "Ferrari."

Gio had taken just a few steps toward the Neurmers when Angela turned away from her husband and appealed to Gio, the mighty Gio who could accomplish anything, with wild, desperate eyes. Gio reached for his phone and quickly punched in two numbers. "Marco, get up on deck! Now! Bring the defibrillator—a guest is down!"

Angela cradled her husband. "Good God, Todd, please hang on! God, please! Todd, please!"

She was gasping for breath. "God, no! Todd! Oh, Todd! Please!"

In her mind they were caught in an enormous dark vortex in the sea. Swirling along with them were all her thoughts for the future: Todd congratulating Courtney at graduation, Todd walking Courtney down the aisle, Todd holding his grandchild, Todd kissing her, Todd holding her, Todd laughing, Todd dancing, Todd with his mischievous grin, Todd being stupid, Todd injuring his ankle, Todd demanding, Todd loving, Todd hurrying, Todd watching TV ...

She managed to pull free from the mental whirlpool for just a moment, and her caregiver instinct took over. She laid him down with tears still streaming down her bright red face and confirmed that he wasn't breathing nor had any pulse. His ventricle was fluttering ineffectively, and no blood or oxygen was moving through his gray and clammy body.

Angela began CPR, though she wasn't providing any breathing aid. She pumped his chest about fifteen times before Marco ran up with an automatic defibrillator. Gio gently pulled Angela aside as Marco ripped off Todd's white shirt and quickly pasted two pads on either side of his heart.

It didn't take the machine long to make a determination and send an enormous jolt of electricity that careened Todd's lifeless body into the air. It was meant to shock the heart back into rhythm, but Todd's heart just fibrillated. The machine fired again and again and again because it didn't like what it was seeing.

The rest of the dinner party had silently gathered behind Angela, who kneeled on the deck as if in prayer. A stunned Ote held Juliana tight. Angela looked intently from the machine to Todd. Her husband was now a tangle of himself as the machine kept firing; he seemed to be staring at the onlookers in white as his head flopped with each dose of electricity.

"Turn the damn thing off!"

Angela lunged forward and tore the probes off her husband's chest. She lay across his body with her arms wrapped under him, kissing him, sobbing, praying her kisses would perform the miracle the defibrillator could not. She saw the fear of impending doom in his eyes. She saw him mouth *I love you* and realized that he knew too.

It was frantic pandemonium as a helicopter landed aboard the yacht. Father Viglianti, Gio, Marco, and Ote ran Todd's body up to the helipad. Within a minute of landing, the helicopter departed with Todd, Angela, and Gio aboard, heading directly to Naples to the same hospital Ciro had just escaped.

All of the guests were dazed, especially Ciro, for he had witnessed firsthand what he missed when the chillingly similar chain of events struck him down just weeks earlier. Shaking and crying, he was hugging Amalia.

They looked back at the dining table still filled with plates of uneaten veal and potatoes garnished with delicate asparagus sprigs, a picture of that wonderful moment now frozen in time and lost forever. The chairs were askew, marking that terrifying birth when they were irrevocably torn from that moment.

Just over an hour later, Angela stumbled out of Todd's hospital room with Gio holding her up. Her eyes were swollen and red as tomatoes, and rivulets of black mascara delineated the lines of grief and wear on her face.

Chapter 18: You Are Changeable II

Neither Ciro nor Amalia could sleep; they couldn't get the image of Angela's horrified face out of their minds. After hours of flopping of the pillows, trying to sleep on their stomachs, backs, and both sides, Amalia broke the silence.

"Ciro?" she whispered, just in case he had somehow found sleep.

"I know—I can't get past it either."

She wriggled into his arms and he spooned her tightly.

"I wish there was something—anything—we could do," Amalia lamented, "but there's nothing, Angela is all alone—so desperately alone."

"*Sí, sí.*"

"She reacted just as I did when I saw you all but dead on the beach. I know how devastated she must be to have someone she loves so dearly ripped from her life."

Her tears splashed on Ciro's arm. He pulled her in even closer and caressed her soft, wet cheek.

"And their daughter—can you imagine? She's out with her friends, not a care in the world, and someone will pay her a surprise visit … She'll be happy to see them until she notices their pain …"

"Let's try not to think of this, Amalia. It's tragic, no doubt about it, but Todd's in heaven now. His wife and daughter will eventually find comfort in that, and his life will live on through his daughter and her memories. Of course she'll be crushed, but she will recover. Look at Ote; he made it through his father's death."

"But he had the love of his family and friends. Angela's all alone. It's just so cruel. Why wouldn't God intervene? Why does he help some but not others? Todd was always smiling—

he loved life, his family, and God. Why punish them all, God? And so soon after you almost left us, when the wounds were just mending, the despicable taste of fear and desperation were finally washed away?"

"Yes. God intervened on my behalf by providing Angela to take over my care, and now her husband's gone, just like that."

"So how are you doing? You act like everything is okay but I know that it's not. What's going on in your head?"

"*Sí,* I know and I should have confided in you, but I'll see my way through this, and I didn't want you to think that I'm a broken man. You deserve not to have to worry about me, and you deserve to never have to go through what Dr. Angela's going through now. The whole time I was sick, it was easy for me, I just slept, but now I know what I caused you ..."

"Stop."

"This is just how I'm thinking. I wish that I weren't but do you want me to lie? I can't stop thinking I might drop again at any moment."

"Oh Ciro, don't you listen to your doctors? You are better now than you ever have been—just follow their orders!" It occurred to her that some of those orders were from Dr. Angela, and her tears grew to fountains, choking off her words.

Ciro kissed her jaw. "Let's discuss this in the morning. I'll be fine. We should pray for the Neurmers." While in prayer they finally managed to drift off to sleep.

Ciro stood naked the next morning in front of their large circular mirror and dripped shower water onto the faded blue ceramic tiles. He had already run his towel through his hair, which stood up straight like a cartoon character's who had been shocked by electricity.

In his mind, the mirror rotated like a fan on lowest speed. Whenever he saw himself now, his image was always twisting and turning.

He had always taken health for granted. At the very least

he would have expected his body to warn him. Now he no longer knew who he was. Standing there naked in front of the mirror, he wondered why a flower was a flower and a weed a weed.

To him, some weeds looked like flowers and even had the flowers to prove it. Flowers lured. To him, some flowers looked like weeds and yet they never flowered. Weeds were ugly. He didn't see himself in the spinning mirror so he concluded he must be a weed. He didn't consider that weeds were hardy and sustainable and without poisons mostly impossible to exterminate.

"Ciro... Ciro... are you ignoring me?" He couldn't see her standing behind him because the mirror was still spinning. She spanked him, startling him to reality. Then she grabbed the hairbrush off the counter and prepared to groom her man.

"Sorry, I was just thinking about last night."

"Get dressed and join me out on the couch, we need to talk." Amalia gave him another spank and strode out of the bathroom.

She waited for Ciro with her feet on the couch, her knees tucked up to her chin and her arms wrapped around her shins. She tried to think of the best approach to bring the real Ciro back and decided that she should be unrehearsed and speak from her heart.

Ciro stepped out of the bedroom. "Nice souvenir the surgeon left me, huh?" gesturing to the long pink incision neatly zippered down his sternum.

"It shall serve as your reminder that you are no longer a smoker."

"I miss them!"

"Come sit by me, Ciro. You have me very worried, and it's time that we talk about our fears. We need to hear Gio's words and start living again, but we can't do that without the truth that comes from our hearts! Remember how comfortable and honest we were with each other, we trusted each other. We shared in both joy and crisis, but we always shared, and I miss that terribly."

She would have continued if she could, but instead she buried her head between her knees and wept silently.

"Oh sweet Amalia, I do nothing but cause you grief, and I know what you say is true. I don't wish to be this way, trust me, but I remain so tormented. It hurts me to see how my torment hurts you, that I am the cause of your pain, and I have no idea on how to make it better. Every morning I hope the torment will have passed but instead it grows. I do my best to mask it but of course I fail when I'm with you—"

"Stop!"

Amalia uncoiled her body and stamped her feet against the floor. "Stop it with your self-pity. And how dare you tell me how I feel? When did you stop asking and start knowing? You fool no one except maybe Ote, who's also off in la-la land. I've discussed it with your parents and your sister, and we all agree that you're miserable despite your fake smile, yet you refuse to talk about this with anyone! You throw us out like garbage for your own selfish, thoughtless reasons!"

"They're hardly selfish. I only think of others, not myself … I think of the pain I have caused, how I have disrupted so many lives …"

"Listen to yourself, Ciro. Don't you hear what you are saying? Don't you understand that you made it? We *all* made it; we've been blessed by your recovery. Don't you understand what Mrs. Neurmer would do to speak with her husband now, but she can't …"

Amalia's tears again stopped her mid-sentence.

Ciro laid his head down onto Amalia's lap and saw the truth of what she said. For the first time in more than a month he actually thought and considered. He thought about the great memories he was fortunate enough to have with the Neurmers while they vacationed over the span of several years.

He remembered brief snippets like Todd tossing his

daughter Courtney into the air to splash into the sea, the Neurmers playing paddleball, throwing the Frisbee ... he could see Todd fearlessly dive off a rock into the transparent sea and trying to encourage his daughter to do the same. He was a pretty good diver.

Or Todd playing soccer one summer with the local kids on the beach and cracking skulls as he went up for a header—that was one of the few times Ciro saw Angela scold him. As he was thinking about this, tears pooled on his chin before dripping onto his fresh scar. These tears would heal his heart, finally. Even from beyond earthly life, a Neurmer had resurrected Ciro.

"I'm so grateful to have you in my life, Amalia. I don't want to miss any more time with you—one never knows, do they? Tragedy can strike at any time. Thank God Ote was there for me—he's always been there for me. But I worry that he hasn't really forgiven me for my outburst. But I'm sure that I love you now more than ever. Let's move on and celebrate Todd's life with our own life, build a family so I can watch you watch me playing with our children. We have still so much to do, so let's begin today!"

Amalia heard it in his voice and saw it in his eyes—she had her old Ciro back. She was smothering him with kisses when they heard several knocks on his front door.

"Who's there?" Ciro questioned.

"It's Isabella." His sister had been a frequent guest lately.

"Get the door," said Ciro. "Let me tidy up a bit and grab a shirt." He was still a little self-conscious of his scar, but it too would fade away soon.

He went into the bathroom to brush his teeth but didn't acknowledge that the round mirror had stopped rotating and landed on "Your life returns!" But he did notice that his teeth were less stained from nicotine. He celebrated by high-fiving his image in the mirror as his burdens slipped away to find another host.

When he returned to the living room, Amalia and Isabella were discussing last night's terrible tragedy. Ciro gave them both a quick kiss and bolted for the door.

With his old step restored, Ciro set out to find Ote to repair their friendship. He pulled out his cell phone. "Hey where are you?"

"Down at the beach, working. Why, what's up?"

"I'll be down within five minutes. We need to talk."

"Did I mention I was at work?"

"You did, and I know what you do for a living. But it's time to start living for real again. I'll see you shortly." He thought about his cardiologist's instructions and corrected himself: "You know, I think I'll walk down. Give me twenty-five minutes."

Ote had seemed even more dismissive than usual. He wasn't even being clever about it. Never mind, this wasn't the first time the two had sparred. Ciro knew better than anyone that Ote would come around soon.

On the other hand, Ote hadn't liked his friend's happy tone. Ciro was obviously on his way to claim his half of the fortune. Last night's tragedy must have jolted his memory. Or more likely, he'd decided get his grubby hands on the prize before it was too late.

Either way, Ote was prepared and in fact welcomed this inquisition. He had been preparing for this encounter for days; his dejection would finally make sense once he explained that the disk had been stolen. He would describe in great detail his search for it, though he had yet to stumble upon a lead.

Ciro took the same route down as they had the night of his heart attack, though he didn't remember that trip. He carefully negotiated the unevenly carved rock steps that zigzagged between the homes of Praiano from above the coastal road to the sea.

His real smile, his signature smirk, had returned, and he was all but skipping. As he walked down the narrow steps between the tightly spaced villas, he saw the early risers putting laundry on lines, watering their plants, or sweeping their terraces. "*Buon giorno, Signora Rispoli. È una bella giornata!*" he called out as Mrs. Rispoli, an elderly lady in her seventies who still managed the steps, hung out her sheets to dry. She would usually scoff at Ciro but lit up when she saw him.

"*Ciao*, Ciro!"

Farther down and around a zag, "*Ciao, ciao Signora Galani! È una bella giornata!*" Then next not that much later near the zig, "*Signora Cammarota, come stai?*" The brief encounters didn't slow his pace and his spirits were lifting with every step down. He missed these stairs and couldn't remember the last time he'd taken them—since getting out of the hospital, he'd been relying on his worn-out car.

He appreciated the journey, taking it slower, enjoying the individuality of each stacked villa and the individuality of Praiano's residents—in Signora Cammarota's case, her formidable breasts, though for the most part he had long since stopped noticing such things.

As he neared the marina, he stopped by the Africana. He had so many fond memories from when Ote worked there, both before he met Amalia and just before they closed it. He could picture Ote in his black trousers and white long-sleeved dress shirt, sometimes smiling and other times absorbed by his duties.

Ciro laughed as he remembered how they used to play games with unsuspecting female tourists when they were younger, back when most of the women were older than they were, back when there was only one way to score.

Ciro loved and missed Gennaro too. He had only seen him twice in more than a month. He hadn't even noticed until just this second how much he had been ignoring in his life—he hadn't even thought of Gennaro or really anybody since he realized how terrible he felt for yelling at Amalia and Ote.

Since then, he had been blankly considering his own

vulnerability, tuning out the conversations that he was supposed to be participating in. He pretended to be cheerful, but he was not an experienced mask wearer.

Ote, however, was quite experienced. As Ciro rounded the rocky cliff, Ote was retelling the story of Todd's death to the fifth person this morning: Danilo Potenza, a cook at one of the tourist restaurants. Danilo had recently finished school and was a decent enough cook, despite his young age.

"Hang on, Ote—is that a ghost I see?"

It was the first time Ciro, usually a regular, had been to La Praia since his heart attack. This didn't even occur to him, he was so happy to see his friends. "Potenza!" he exclaimed. "*Come stai?*" Ciro was bright-eyed as he hugged Danilo and gave him two quick pecks on the cheeks. "You look great!"

"As do you! What a night you had! Ote was just telling me—crazy!"

"It's like it didn't happen, a dream …"

"So sad! You knew Todd didn't you?"

"Yes, of course. Not that well, but I'd seen him around forever …"

"He was a great man!" Ote joined in, his espresso lifted to the heavens.

"I'll take one of those," said Ciro, "but make mine an Americano."

"I'll grab you one," said Danilo. "I'll make us all one … for the American." He went around to behind the bar and mixed one part espresso with two parts hot water, the American blend. When he got back, Ciro and Ote were sitting at a table overlooking the beach and wondering how Todd's family was getting along. When Danilo sat down, Ciro lifted his glass.

"To Todd and Angela," he said. "May Todd be fishing heaven's seas, and may Dr. Angela and her family forgive God as we all must forgive. *Arrivederci*, Todd!"

They clanked their glasses, sipped their Americanos, and

grimaced at its diluted taste. "And to you, Ote," Ciro continued, "who I love with all my newly repaired heart."

"Danilo, we need to get things prepped for the lunch crowd," Salvatore called from inside the restaurant.

"Boss is calling," Danilo said with a shrug.

Ote anxiously watched Danilo return to work. Suddenly he didn't want to be alone with Ciro, who was sure to accuse him of stealing the treasure. The old Ciro wouldn't have let him get away with it, nor would this new Ciro who was promising to be every bit as formidable. And the old Ciro was not always nice.

Ciro looked Ote in the eyes. "I stopped by the Africana on my way down and relived a lot of great memories. So sad it's closed now."

Ote was sure that Ciro was staring him down, trying to determine whether he'd flinched at the mention of the Africana.

Of course! That's why Ciro had taken the steps. What a brilliant way to introduce the subject. That no-good conniving snoop!

"It's a real shame," Ote replied blandly, though he couldn't look his friend in the eye. "Terrible, really, so many people out of work. Speaking of, when are you going to return to work?"

"Soon enough. Piccoleto is running the place and doing a great job. Apparently people are even praising the food for the first time. I guess most people don't even miss me. They are glad that Amalia's back though. I think she thinks she's the boss with me gone."

"What made you stop by the Africana?" Now it was Ote doing the measuring.

"I didn't stop long, just remembering how much fun we shared there. So many great memories!"

Ote heard him stress his words *remembering* and *memories*— trying to provoke him, obviously.

"Fabiano was in town over the weekend," said Ote. "He visited you while you were in the hospital—before you woke up with all these *memories*."

"Yeah, I know. He stopped by after I woke up too, though I don't think I could tell you what we discussed. I was still pretty much sauced."

Ah ha! To Ote's ear, Ciro seemed to put extra emphasis on the first syllable of *discutere* (Italian for "discussed"). Now he was certain that Ciro knew.

"Maybe I should move out of town too," said Ote. "Get away, make a fresh start. I'll never be able to afford the things Juliana deserves working here."

"You can't move away, Ote. I need you, you saved my life. You've got to get over what I said when I coming out of my coma. I love you like a brother!"

This reply confused Ote, as there was not a hint that Ciro remembered their great discovery.

"Yes, I know," Ote said bitterly. "We have many great memories, don't we? Some not so long ago—isn't that right?"

"Relax, Ote. I don't know what I can say to convince you, but I'll do whatever it takes!"

"I'm over it! How many times do I have to tell you that? Good God! Why don't you just tell me why you're really here and save your breath?"

This outburst initiated an outbreak of hand-waving, finger-pointing, and livid faces.

"Listen," shouted Ciro as he leaped to his feet. "I see how you talk to me; I see your little smirks. How many jams have I gotten you out of? I'm not like you—I speak from my heart. *That's* why I'm really here, to fix things between us. What the hell's up with you, Ote?"

"What the hell's wrong with *me*? You call me a dear friend but you test our friendship because you don't trust me. You know the truth, and yet you just test me!"

"I have no idea what you're talking about. Testing you?

What the hell does that mean?"

Ote flipped over the small table, spraying Ciro with the Americanos. Danilo and Salvatore ran out to break things up.

"You no good bastard! Are you nuts?" Ciro gestured at his stained clothes with a look of utter disbelief. He stepped toward Ote and Danilo pulled him back.

"Guys, guys! Come on, you're friends!"

"He's no friend of mine!" Ote spat, wrenching his arm free from Salvatore's grasp. "I can't wait to leave this damned place and all you idiots behind forever!"

Ciro looked down again at his coffee stained outfit and smiled as Ote stormed off, believing it had gone better than expected. He understood now that Ote was hiding something, but had no idea what and wasn't that concerned. Ciro knew how Ote's moods swung on a pendulum—a pendulum that was usually stuck on the happy side of the arc, although it was now stuck now on the unhappy side. Ciro knew it was best to shove the pendulum toward the apogee of unhappiness, so that it would rebound with accelerated speed.

Ote stormed off toward St. Gennaro basilica. He hoped that Father Viglianti would be there to hear his confession and fill him with inspiration so that his wicked thoughts would have no room to return and gain strength. He took out his frustration on his motorcycle gearbox, barely clutching each shift. He was mostly confused by a vengeful, suspicious greed, but he was also beginning to doubt whether he might be wrong about Ciro. Maybe his friend actually didn't remember the disk.

Viglianti was sitting on his small terrace overlooking the sea and working on a crossword puzzle. He was out of uniform in his plum shorts and a Roma SSC blue t-shirt with his toes waggling in the breeze. He'd been stumped by twenty-three across and was trying to fill in the intersecting downs when he heard the knock on his front door.

Wondering who might be calling unannounced, he stopped briefly at his desk near the terrace doors to check his planner and confirm that he hadn't forgotten an appointment. Anything might have happened to one of his parishioners—by this point in his life he had seen it all.

Most of the time he found these interruptions not to be a matter of faith but a waste of time, though he did try to give them some perfunctory help before he sent them back out to fend for themselves. Perhaps unsurprisingly, the number of interruptions to his quiet home life had steadily declined as the years went by.

"Sorry to bother you, Father!" Ote said, a bit breathless. "I need to speak with someone before I too have a heart attack. Can you spare me a few moments of your time?"

Ote gave him an imploring smile, his closed lips barely rounding up. He used this expression often and naturally.

"Come on in, Ote. I expected to see you sooner. I've been worried about you!"

The priest led Ote through the front room used for entertaining and onto the terrace. Ote sat facing away from the sea, toward the nearby gleaming basilica.

"Father, forgive me for I am with sin though I can't describe it. I'm not sure which commandment I have broken but I have surely committed a sin that's causing me such pain!"

"Describe the pain and what causes it, Ote."

"It's difficult for me to say this but it's Ciro. After all I have done for him, not just recently but over the years, he thanks me by testing me. We shared a little secret before he had his heart attack. In fact I think the secret caused his heart attack so now I am afraid to tell him."

"How do you know he is testing you?"

"He taunted me with snide remarks just to see if I would react."

"Tell me how he taunts you."

"He mentions clues or stresses words when he talks. And he tried to attack me today, just like when he first woke up!"

"Is it possible that you have misread your friend? I don't

see him as someone who would taunt you or test you. I heard about what he said to you—he's deeply troubled by that and he has his own issues."

Ote stood and turned toward the sea with his back to Viglianti. "Deep within me I know that I'm misreading him and that he really has forgotten about our secret. Yet something else within me argues against the facts!"

"Why not just tell him? And is this secret really so powerful that it causes heart attacks?"

Viglianti was now looking to push this thing along so that he could resume his crossword puzzle.

"Well, we found something that has just a little bit of value and we both got really excited because it seems we never have good fortune. But it's really not that valuable at all." Ote coughed nervously. "It's something no one would even miss. You see, we caught a fish and I ended up cashing it in but didn't split the money with Ciro. You're right as always. It's crazy that I let this secret plague me."

"So when are you going to talk to him?"

Father Viglianti realized that Ote had created quite a dilemma for himself. He had nearly laughed when Ote mentioned that the secret was a fish. What Ote had disclosed before his hopeless attempt to sweep it back under the rug answered a lot of questions that Viglianti had entertained for over a month now. He doubted that he would report this new information to his superior, at least for now. He was almost happy for them.

"Right away, Father. I feel a huge burden lifted already, thank you. I'll let you get back to your crossword puzzle. You know, Ciro and I always did the crossword puzzles together, and I haven't done one since his heart attack."

"I've been having trouble with forty-four down." Viglianti picked up the paper and read the clue aloud: "'Penned *The Deep*?' I remember the story. It was about those people that discovered a fortune's worth of drugs of some sort out to sea, but I cannot remember the author … I think he wrote that shark book too …"

"Is it eight letters like Benchley?"

"That's right!"

Ote was too proud of himself for getting the answer to catch what the priest was hinting at.

Father Viglianti was barely able to contain his enthusiasm as he led Ote back the same way he had entered. He beamed as he opened his front door. "Don't spend it all at once—the knowledge that is. Spread it out over time so you don't get so worked up over nothing. Go and enjoy all of God's gifts. And say hello to Ciro!"

Viglianti shut the door behind him and walked back to the terrace. He leaned over the wrought-iron railing and looked out to sea with his back to the church. "Those lucky, lucky boys. What a twist of fate!"

He laughed until he buckled over. What a find, worthy of a heart attack! He intended to keep it a secret from all.

Chapter 19: In Health and Virtue

Ciro was standing at the back of the eight-meter orange passenger boat taking him from La Praia to One Fire. The wind billowed his black hair behind him as he took in the stunning coastline views. Pino, his employee and captain, sat back in his captain's chair and steered the boat with his right foot. Pino looked back at him and saluted.

"It's great to have you back, Ciro!"

"It's a great day, Pino. Just look around—we have it all, right here!"

"The view's even better with you in foreground smiling. It was a very difficult time. You scared us!"

"Yeah, I know. Me too. I'm finally starting to feel normal again."

"What's up with those stains on your shorts?"

Ciro laughed. "You finally noticed, did you? Very observant. It happened this morning, when I finally realized how good I have it and spilled coffee all over on myself. It's like the Americans say—I woke up and smelled the coffee!"

Pino deserted his post and hugged Ciro for several seconds. "Let's make the best of all our time, Ciro. I'm so glad you are back with us!"

"I'd better take over from here. You're going to crash into those cliffs. I'm still fragile, and you aim to kill me yet!"

"Have the doctors cleared you for captaining this vessel?"

"The authorities certainly wouldn't approve of you splitting my head against those rocks!" Ciro grabbed the helm and turned hard to his right, toppling Pino into the wooden bench seating that encircled the rear three-quarters of the boat.

"Wow that was a close one!" Pino said sarcastically. "In another five minutes or so we would have rammed those

rocks! Thank God for Ciro and his quick thinking!"

With a cheesy grin Ciro whipped the boat back toward the rocks and pretended to have near-miss after near-miss until finally—and mercifully, Pino would have argued—Ciro's phone chimed. It was Ote, and Ciro shut the engine off and glided to the quiet of the sea.

"It's Gerardo." Ciro put the phone on speaker and motioned Pino over. "Well, if it isn't Ote!"

"Hey listen—sorry about that, man. Really didn't mean to douse you in coffee."

Pino pointed at Ciro's shorts and feigned a silent laugh. Ciro gave him a quick wink and smiled.

"No problem. It was an accident. I've been trying to figure out what you were talking about back there—me testing you, me remembering—and I don't understand?"

"Oh, you will soon enough. Where are you now? I'm about to make today a great day for you—the best of your life, to be sure!"

Ciro looked toward Pino and circled his ear with his right index finger. "Cuckoo," he mouthed.

"It already is, Ote, just because I get to hear your voice. It's so soothing, like a splash of fresh watered-down coffee!"

"Don't worry about my voice, idiot. Just wait till I show you what you'll see for the first time since your weak heart failed. Should I tell you now so that you will hurry on over here and stop wasting time?"

"Did you slam a few drinks since I last just saw you?"

With that Pino blew his cover and laughed loud enough to be heard.

"Are you nuts, man? Who's with you?"

"Ah Ote, it's only Pino. Can I see the big surprise too?"

"It's nothing, really. I was ... well ... Gennaro can juggle the ball now for three minutes nonstop and Ciro was just saying how much he wanted to see him so I thought ..."

"That would be great, man. I need to stop in to One Fire

for an hour or so then I could meet you guys where. But why isn't Gennaro at Juliana's mom's?"

"Just meet me at my house—I'll see you then. Hey, I have to run. *Ciao*, Pino."

Just over an hour later, Ciro pounded on the door to Ote's home. "Who dares to beat the mighty record of Ciro?" he boomed.

From the alley behind him, Melissa Pelliccia, Ote's twenty-four-year-old neighbor answered.

"Ciro Pane, will nothing keep you down? Come over here and let me see you!"

"Ah, Signora Pelliccia! Excuse me, I am too loud. How are you?"

Ciro walked toward the beautiful woman with arms extended, his cheeks rounded as he greeted her with a delicate kiss on each side of her face.

"I'm back! Did you miss me?"

"Ciro Pane—miss you? Certainly not, but I'm glad to see you. I was just watering Mama's garden. Would you care to help?"

With perfect timing, Ote opened his apartment door. "Leave Melissa alone! She doesn't need to be bothered with your lechery today. Come, I need your help."

Ote motioned Ciro into his home with an awkward smile of good-bye to his neighbor and shut his door behind Ciro.

"Who here wishes to challenge the mighty Ciro's record?"

"Gennaro's not even here. That was a lie, though he can keep the ball in the air for nearly three minutes. You're about to realize a dream—now sit." Ote pointed toward the faded yellow wicker loveseat.

Ote remained standing, pacing and peering out his windows as if confirming that this conversation would be top secret. Finally he let out a huge sigh of relief and a smile spread across his face. Ciro was amused to see that Ote was shaking with excitement and wondered what might be next from his predictably unpredictable friend.

"Should we be whispering?" Ciro joked.

"With your big mouth we should be, that's for sure. First, don't ever put me on speakerphone again—ever! You could have ruined everything! Next, you must promise me as you promised on the night of your heart attack, that you're not to tell anyone about what I'm going to show you—and that includes Amalia. Please understand that I'm serious, man!"

As serious as Ote tried to look, he kept undercutting his message with a wide smile.

"Damn, man, what's going on? You need to sit down and relax and tell me what's up."

Instead Ote started flailing his arms, dancing to some song in his head. "We're rich! We're rich! We're rich!" He pulled Ciro off the loveseat and gave him a bear hug.

Ciro did his best to play along, but with no idea of what Ote was celebrating, his dancing was a little less exuberant.

"Do you know how difficult it's been for me to keep our secret? It's been a torture! And you really have no idea, none?"

"I think perhaps you've lost your mind, but that's nothing new."

"Follow me!"

Ote swaggered toward the back of the apartment, grabbed a wooden dining chair, and placed it in the hallway under a wooden panel that accessed the attic. He stepped onto the chair, slid the panel above him onto the attic floor, and then hoisted himself up into the hole.

"Do you think you are strong enough to lift yourself up here?" he asked with his legs dangling from the opening.

"It looks like you're leading me into some sort of sinister trap, but I'll play along. I'm still at half-strength, but that's more enough to take care of you!"

Ciro tried several times to pull himself up, but his arm muscles were still too atrophied. He looked up at Ote, grinning.

"If this isn't a message from God to run from this house before you attack me then I don't know what is. How else to explain this sudden onset of weakness!"

Ote didn't say a word in reply. Ciro heard him moving boxes around, and finally Ote reappeared with a smile that seemed to span the entire opening. With an abracadabra motion from behind his back, he rained down bundles of five-hundred-Euro bank notes that thudded onto Ciro's head. Ciro attempted to protect himself with his hands and arms as Ote laughed wildly and pelted his friend with showers of purple bills.

"Stop it! Are you completely nuts? I'm still fragile, can't you—" Ciro stopped short as he saw for the first time what Ote had used in his attack. He bent down and snatched up a bundle. He rifled through the currency, touching it, examining with a treasury agent's scrutiny, even smelling the bundle. It smelled real.

Ote scrambled back down to the hallway and stood next to his friend with bundles of five-hundred-Euro notes surrounding them.

"It's all real, nothing counterfeit. There are boxes of bundles up there. Here, get back on the chair and I'll help push you up!"

"Where'd all this come from?"

"You can ask your questions later. For now, just go up and see for yourself. Quickly, we don't have much time!"

With the help of adrenaline Ciro didn't need Ote to pull himself through the opening. Ote swiftly gathered up the bundles from the floor and stepped onto the chair.

"Here, take these—we have to put them back!"

Soon Ote joined Ciro in the cramped attic full of boxes. A single light bulb dangling from the roof gave them just enough light to let them sidle past a row of boxes that were filled with holiday decorations. Ote pointed to four large boxes tucked behind them.

"They're all full of five-hundred Euro bills! Not sure exactly how much because I haven't counted it yet, but millions to be certain!"

Ote carefully placed the bundles back into the open box and shut it carefully. Then he stacked some other boxes on top of the ones containing their treasure.

"That must have been a big tuna, Ote!" Ciro tried to joke as they climbed back down out of the attic. Ote secured the trap door, making micro-adjustments to center it perfectly over the hole before returning the chair to the dining room and then joining Ciro in the living room.

"Half of that is yours, Ciro! We found it the night before your heart attack!"

"Where'd we find it?"

"Out to sea, we found a large disk and hid it that night in the Africana grotto. Then the next night we went to open up the disk and found all this money! It nearly killed you on the spot!"

"I can't remember any of it! That cash is ours? Are you sure it's not counterfeit?"

"It's real and it's ours!"

They joined in dance again, Ciro dancing for real this time, whirling and gyrating. "Slow down, man!" said Ote. "You need to calm down before your heart blows up again!"

Ciro's joy spewed like a geyser. Tears were running down his glowing cheeks and his heart was racing but holding strong. "They fixed my heart. Tell me more!"

"We were fishing, we thought we were about to land a yellowfin but it turned out to be a grouper. Then we saw the disk and pulled it ashore. I got rid of it already."

"How'd you get the money here? Does anyone else know? How do you know it's real? How—"

"Slow down, I'll tell you everything! I moved the money here a little at a time. I had hidden the money behind rocks and in the walls of the grotto. And it's real—the disk was very sophisticated and well built. Who'd build a high-priced disk and put fake money in it? Too bad you can't remember it!"

"And I take it there were no reports of missing disks full of money? As happy as we are, someone must be equally furious."

"I've been very careful and haven't spent any of it. I waited to tell you because I wanted to make sure you were well enough to handle the news this time. It's been killing me to keep this secret from you. Of course I thought—but just for a moment—that maybe you remembered and were testing me to see if I am honest."

"Oh, so that's what this morning was about?"

"Yeah, well maybe a little, but mostly I didn't want to risk giving you another heart attack! Can you believe how rich we are? It's like a dream that turned into a nightmare and back into a dream!"

"We can't just all of a sudden start buying new cars or flashing five-hundred Euro notes around town. We need to think carefully about how to not get discovered. People are looking for this."

Chapter 20: Driven On and Weighted Down, Always Enslaved

Alessio, Aprajita, and Ramesh were walking on the Via degli Ausoni near their home in the San Lorenzo district of Rome, going the wrong way on a one-way street filled with the hangover-dazed eyes of backpack-toting students on their Monday morning march to campus.

"Don't you think he might be just a little too young?" Aprajita asked. "Maybe after we get him out of diapers?"

"It's never too early! It's not cricket, that's for sure. I won't be rocketing dangerously hard rubber balls at him!"

It was their first time out to the soccer field, and Alessio expected to witness a Serie A star in the making, given the natural skills Ramesh had demonstrated kicking a miniature soccer ball through the doorways in the apartment and his mother's prowess on the tennis court.

"The ball's bigger than he is! If you hurt him, I'll never speak to you again! Now go get your son before he runs into traffic!"

Ramesh was wobbling through the crowd with the soccer ball clutched in his hands. Alessio took several exaggerated long steps and lifted his boy above his head.

"Ramesh wants to be a goalkeeper? No, no, no—you have much too much speed and ball skills to use your hands! You can only you use your hands in tennis!"

"Tennis, Papa!"

Ramesh laughed, and with decent forehand mechanics swung his right hand hard and through his Papa's right cheek.

"Tennis, Papa!"

Alessio lowered his son and gave him a kiss. "Yes, that's how you play tennis! Very good!"

He looked over at Aprajita, expecting to see her laughing, expecting anything but tears. She smiled at him when she saw his concern.

"I just cannot believe what a miracle it is that we found each other ... Here I am in Rome, no longer alone ... and the thought of Ramesh without you brings my tears."

"Or maybe were you looking at me and seeing an old man and wondering what you've gotten yourself into!"

"That's why I cry myself to sleep at night!"

Alessio wrapped his arms around Aprajita and gently wiped away the tears upon her cheek.

"Only God could orchestrate our reunion," he said. "I love you so much—so very, very much!"

He stared into her eyes, capturing a glimpse of her spirit, her being, her energy penetrating him.

"Aprajita, there is no one I desire more than you, there never will be. You could make me the happiest man on earth!"

"Oh Alessio, I'd do anything that brings you happiness— anything!"

"Will you take me for a husband? Will you be my most caring, thoughtful, beautiful, and exciting wife?"

Aprajita lightly touched his face with her trembling fingertips, then slid her hand around to the back of his head and pulled him in for a firm kiss. Ramesh, having lost all patience, swung his arm with all his might into Alessio's shin.

"What about my ring?" Aprajita asked with her classic arched grin. "It's no wonder Ramesh struck you—even he knows that I should have a ring!"

"More than your beauty, it's your quick wit that I love most about you! You'll get your ring, my love, but I didn't know I was going to propose to you today. Something unexplainable came over me!"

Alessio took the soccer ball from Ramesh and kicked it high and far into the grassy practice fields. He grabbed Aprajita by her waist, hoisted her into the air, and slowly lowered her toward him for one last kiss. Then he sprinted toward the ball to retrieve it.

Aprajita knelt down and took both of Ramesh's hands. "You are very lucky to have a father like Alessio," she told him in Gujarati. "And I am even luckier!" She lifted him up and spun him in the air. "We are both so lucky!"

Alessio returned with the ball, slightly out of breath.

"I was just telling Ramesh that I wasn't sure that your heart could take such exertion!"

Alessio juggled the soccer ball for several moments before responding. "Are you kidding? I could do this for weeks!"

"Very impressive for a man your age!"

As it turned out, Ramesh's first time on the soccer field was somewhat premature. Alessio tried again and again to gain his son's attention, to teach him to kick the ball with the instep of the foot, not the toes, but each demonstration was interrupted by distractions that only a small child could appreciate: a horn in traffic, a bird, a drifting cloud.

The smell of lavender permeated the marbled bathroom of their home while Ramesh was fast asleep, worn out by the day's energy. Candles rimmed the bathtub's ledges, their flickering light reflecting the champagne bubbles seeking the tops of their glasses. Alessio faced Aprajita, their legs touching beneath the steamy water. He was shampooing her hair with both hands, massaging her thick black hair at the nape of her neck.

"Do you want me to dunk you under the water to rinse the shampoo out of your hair? Or should I run the—?"

"You want to force my head down? It turns me on when you do that, Alessio!"

She slid forward and plunged her head into the water. He furiously scrubbed the soap from her hair and scalp in a burst of shampoo suds coming to the surface. As she finished, he reached for her hand and pulled her up toward him.

Cradling her neck with his bronzed hand, he softly kissed

her with his lips slightly apart. He ever so slightly caressed her bottom lip, and then kissed his way down and around her neck, each kiss more meaningful and deliberate and intentional.

"I float in a state of Ananda," she murmured. "You must never stop."

"Amanda? What is Amanda?"

She curled back around and softly she pressed her hands to the sides of his face.

"A-NAN-da. It is bliss … great happiness. It means that you fulfill all of my desires. Before you I believed what was written, that a state of Ananda was impossible to achieve."

She leaned forward, sliding her hands to the back of his head and neck. Their lips touched and energy flowed from one to the other.

After a minute, Alessio broke the circuit. "From now on I will call you Ananda! You are my Ananda. It shocks me, this love I have for you."

Aprajita gave him a sly grin. "Tonight I want to relive our first night together. When there were no rules! When we exposed ourselves, our desires, our fantasies."

"Hold on tight!"

And with that he lifted her out of the tub. Drips of water mapped their trail out of the bathroom and ended at the foot of their bed.

Chapter 21: I Bring My Bare Back to Your Villainy

Seven years and forty-one days before Ciro and Ote discovered the disk, Giocondo Benvenuto, a distinguished PhD in anthropology from Duke, was sifting through the dusty, rainless earth in Sudan. His close friends back home called him Dr. Dirt Digger. The children here called him Dakka B.

Benvenuto had grown up working as a volunteer, assisting archeologists by painstakingly cleaning artifacts grain by grain with a small paintbrush. He had spent most of his time spent near Pompeii and Herculaneum.

After he graduated, his Catholic devotion brought him to Sudan, where he had convinced a university to support his archeological efforts. His stint in Sudan was fortunately situated between the civil wars, preceding the bedlam and bloody butchery that would follow. He worked out of Abu Hamed, a village tucked into a long sweeping S-turn along the right bank of the Nile. Egypt was to the north, the Red Sea to the east.

For four years he and ten locals worked in the stifling heat, the locals for pennies a day. The excavated site had yielded few treasures, and his benefactors were growing increasingly impatient. Many of his colleagues thought he was crazy to be wasting his efforts in a place where no significant finds had ever been documented.

This, like every day before it, was a new one, Benvenuto noted resolutely. Every day he inspired his poorly paid staff, reiterating that although it was unlikely that they'd make a new discovery, this was how the process worked. It could take years before their efforts returned worthwhile blessings. But in the back of his head, he could hear the rumblings from his sponsors and knew that his time was running out.

Just after a lunch of herbed rice, he was summoned to a

corner tract in their grid by Sarajon Hashampour, the mother of two of his favorite children, Abdikarim and Zeneb. She was actually working off-grid, but by design, at the apogee of the bottom of the "S" in the Nile's sweep just twenty feet from the river's edge. The slightly exposed object looked very foreign to the archeologist. It was obviously an alloy and appeared to be of a very intricate design. Sara had been brushing away all morning as his protocol commanded.

"Outstanding work Sara," said Benvenuto. "We may have something here! Please help your sister while I catalog this find."

Benvenuto tediously excavated around the find for the next three hours, trembling as he exposed more and more. When he removed the "briefcase" from the earth, he found it to be remarkably light, almost weightless.

He carried the case to his hut and placed it on his makeshift desk. There didn't appear to be any latches that would give him access to the contents—if there were any contents at all.

He ran his hands along the surface of the case, searching for the hidden fasteners. Just as he was about to give up, the case suddenly opened, seemingly of its own accord.

Well, well, well … what do we have here?

The case was filled with ancient, neatly stacked parchment. The text was written in Latin. His hands shook as he began to read the first page.

I'm not sure how much longer I will survive; they will find me soon. I am known as Pelagius and I stand in the way of the most powerful. If you are reading this, understand that this work that I intend to write is of the utmost importance to all humanity. This information must be preserved! For what is written herein is written in truth. Although I do not comprehend the code or recognize the symbols it's written in, their instructions were clear …

Four hours later, Benvenuto finally read to the middle of the stack of parchment and found pages upon pages of ones and zeros, millions of ones and zeros in the tiniest of script. It was a binary code that had been written down more than fifteen hundred years ago! The pages were clearly written by the hand of the philosopher Pelagius yet they looked nothing like any of his other works.

For now, Benvenuto skipped the binary-filled pages and continued reading what he could. The instructions were becoming clearer and so was his pain.

A week had passed before he fully realized the implications of his discovery. Then he typed the code into his computer commands as instructed, which took him another week of eighteen-hour days, but in the end his patience and diligence paid off. His computer finally understood. *He* finally understood. The message read:

It was 1,000,000,000 years ago this day that our world became unencumbered by improvident contemplation.

As an experiment, we seeded this planet with all life millions of years before this day and have monitored life here ever since. This serves as a look into our own planet's past. The experiment is ongoing. We will not intervene for another 1,000 years.

But I have returned here to set a new course for this world. I have placed, in recognition of our 1,000,000,000 years of advancing science and health, 1,000,000,000 highly sophisticated computers. It was not our intent to interfere, but you, the reader of this text, were chosen because we feared that this planet would not survive.

The computers are buried at the listed coordinates precisely six feet beneath the surface. The computers are Lelesa stones the size of a pecan nut. Many have likely been unearthed but none discovered.

The computers are voice activated. Simply put the Lelesa stone to one eye and say "Therici-Bojab, Bojab-Therici, Therici, Therici."

This is our gift to this world. The Lelesa stone's database is immense. From 1,000,000 years ago up to this very day, everything has been recorded. You can view anywhere on this planet at any particular time. But this information may not be enough for some, so the Lelesa stone will cleanse the mind of the impurities our planet infected them in the year of Flavius Stilicho.

The nearest Lelesa stone was only four miles away. As a distraction, he thought it best to take Karim and Zeneb, two young children from the village whom he'd grown to love. Not just to help him dig, but to keep him sane for just a little while longer. He was losing his battle with sanity at an accelerated pace.

By God, this must be it, he repeatedly thought to himself after hours of digging, only to watch the sand cave back in time and again. But once he finally had the Lelesa stone in his hand, he put it to his right eye and chanted "Therici-Bojab, Bojab-Therici, Therici, Therici."

Let's travel to Rome, August 1, AD 287, he thought.

"Aurelius Carausius is despicable and I shall gut him myself! Return him alive! Or you too shall perish by my sword!"

"I take great pleasure in your trust, Diocletian!"

It was as though Dakka B was actually in the emperor's audience. He could travel anywhere, anytime simply by thinking of it. The Lelesa rock didn't have a display screen, but it flooded his mind with the senses of smell, touch, and taste as well as sight and sound as if he were actually there.

It was at that moment when his world fell apart. He was lucky to get the kids back to their mother before he started sobbing like a loving husband who had lost his wife to an unforeseen tragedy. The pain shook him to his core. His devotion, his entire life, shattered tragically in an instant, and the damage was irreparable.

This was, however, before he realized that if his devotion had been true, then by default more than ninety percent of the rest of the world's devotions were groundless and false, no matter how passionately and genuinely they were engaged in. This was a matter of fact that no one could argue.

Benvenuto placed a note on his door stating that he had been called away unexpectedly, and for the next few days, he retreated to the darkness and stifling heat of his home to be alone with his crushed thoughts. The pain seared through his soul, which was now lost. The Willy Wonka lyrics "the rowers keep on rowing and there's no earthly way of knowing which direction we are going … the rowers keep on rowing, for the danger must be growing" looped ceaselessly in his head.

On the dusty baking sheet of a floor was a meticulously built yellow pyramid. It was five feet across at its base and also five feet tall, constructed from the wadded-up legal paper that bore his failed attempts at getting the song just right. If he'd had a gun instead of a pen, his body would already be bloated, blue, and lifeless.

Know not-the-choice-in penning!
You might—or naught—be winning!
As there's really no beginning!
For the wheel it keeps on spinning!
Though some will say I 'm sinning!
I even see them vio-lining!
No, none of us are sinning!
And for that we should be grinning!
So now we all "B" winning!

He was especially proud of "vio-lining." Giocondo loved Willy Wonka and he knew that the Oompa Loompas were not rowing as Willy sang—they were spinning a large wheel to propel their psychedelic paddleboat, a stern-wheeler, through the madness of the tunnel.

It took Giocondo another two weeks to recover his resolve, although crippling bouts of depression would periodically attack him for years to come.

He had ordered the site in Sudan, where he had barely escaped with his mind, temporarily shut down, though its closure would soon become permanent as he abandoned his pursuit.

At first he intended to share the facts with the world. How else to show that the world as a whole has issues even if some regions of the planet do not?

He wasn't sure the world could handle the actuality. He barely had. But he believed, in the long run, that the world would prosper from the truth. He considered both long- and short-term strategies from a global perspective, as well as his own perspective.

Humanity lived a divisive world, filled with greed, slaughter, hate and fear of the other. Weapons of mass destruction, roadside bombs, and suicide bombers attested to the passion of regional beliefs and commitments.

In the short run, he was heading to a country within a country. To a multinational organization steeped in history, the largest corporation in the world—ultimately that was where Benvenuto placed the blame. Their tentacles branched around the globe, and their business plan was ingenious. His discovery would end the sale of salvation, no matter the version. He hoped his decision to share this truthful burden, and to share in its wealth, would alleviate the painful thoughts that had consumed him.

On his way to their headquarters, he stopped at the obelisk and reflected, as he was knowledgeable about such things. Around AD 40, Caligula ordered the Forum demolished and this particular obelisk transferred to Rome. Caligula placed it on the *spina*—every wheel needs a *spina*, which ran along the center of the Circus of Nero, where it presided over Nero's daily brutal games, Christian executions optional.

With truth in hand, he contemplated the genius of the deceit. Over time, the genius was modified to reflect current market conditions, as he now understood. Their business plan was elastic.

From a regional perspective, the United States dominated in diversity with thousands of unique brands that had segmented from the original creator and global market dominator.

A global flight plan showing departures to paradise demonstrated that the United States was blessed with airports clumped roughly every block. So many captains! Most regions had one or two departing flights. Giocondo could see this now.

The items for consumption were entirely different, but they all utilized a marketing plan that was implemented at birth. All offered their variety of salvation with offers along the lines of "I'll gladly pay you Tuesday for a hamburger today." Unshakable, despite all of the shakes, by passing around the collection basket asking for gifts today in exchange for the promise of a future eternal paradise that surely awaited those dutifully gifting devotees. Their guarantee had yet to be challenged since unsurprisingly, not one spirit had returned from the dead to seek damages for this breach of contract.

Giocondo intended to divert these fraudulent gifts in an out of court settlement that he would negotiate on his own behalf.

Last night in his hotel room, he calculated the global assets of the various multinational businesses at more than €10,000,000,000.000, though he had no supporting evidence for this estimate. With the same thoroughly baseless financial analysis, he determined that nearly €1,000,000,000 was the weekly global cash flow streaming into the myriad multinational organizations. He figured that it was best to take his share monthly rather than weekly—less hassle that way, he thought.

He arrived at their global headquarters prepared. He was not certain that he would walk out alive. No one else was privy to the truth, so he had a contingency plan that would be triggered if he didn't report back within the next seventy-two hours. This comforted him as he entered the facility unannounced, seeking an audience with the CEO. He had a plan but no appointment. Had he sought an appointment none would have been given, for he didn't have the clout. That would change soon.

He was greeted by an employee who lacked the wherewithal to make it happen. Giocondo didn't want to make the truth public but he had known that he would have to start somewhere. Without sharing his discovery, he was able to meet with the employee's superior. This gave him hope that he could get through several more layers of middle managers before the need to share the truth became imperative.

Soon into his discussion with this second employee, it became obvious to the archeologist that he would see the impact the truth had on this devotee to the corporation soon. The man was clearly about to dismiss Benvenuto and return to his duties, and the archeologist was still countless layers in the chain of command below the CEO.

"Thank you for taking your time to meet with me. As I told the gentleman before, I believe that it's best if you take me to your superior immediately. My business here is of the utmost importance. But the proof I bear is not for your eyes, sir. I hope that I convey this truth by my demeanor, my confidence—"

"I can't just take you to see my superior. As you must know, this is a very busy place—"

"Please, you really don't understand. This is of no concern to you, and it's of no concern to your superior either. I must meet with your highest office, and I'm not really asking. I can assure you, if you insist on seeing the truth I'll make a firm believer out of you. And if you really *believe*, you will be devastated, and you don't want your superiors to know that you know!"

"I'm sorry Dr. Benvenuto, but I really must—"

"I'm sorry, sir, but I knew somebody must be the first. I'm not in the mood to argue with you or anyone else here in this despicable office. Your CEO knows, and now you will too."

Giocondo removed the Lelesa rock from his dusty satchel. He saw the man's queer expression of disbelief, then the first quiver, and then heard his quavering voice quack.

I tried to warn you, but you didn't have faith in me, did you, Giocondo thought. Life drained from the man, who looked suddenly bleached and emaciated. He returned with a more senior manager in seemingly no time. And so the process repeated itself.

Within thirty minutes of his arrival at the global headquarters, Giocondo was escorted to the office of the CEO, who already looked pained. He had been forewarned, of course.

Giocondo paid close attention to the CEO's demeanor as a senior management official anxiously, though firmly, advised the man with a prepared and a practiced speech. He found the CEO's reaction reassuring and, interestingly, also practiced.

Benvenuto had moved into the massive office with purpose, dismissing any thoughts of greeting the esteemed CEO with the pageantry that had always been afforded him. He walked in pissed off. He had even fantasized about using the CEO's desk as his urinal before uttering a word. Just step right in and start peeing on his desk. Thankfully he did not satisfy that desire.

When the CEO extended his hand, Giocondo ignored him, instead flopping into a regal, high-backed chair and staring the man down.

"First of all, I want to say that you sicken me, you really do—"

"You're a smart man—do you blame us? Can't you imagine the carnage without us?"

"You're the cause of it! You and your competitors. I know they know too! And please don't waste my time. I'm not here to debate with you! It's pretty simple. Actions will take place if I fail to check in—everyone will know. You're smart enough to understand this, aren't you?"

The CEO just nodded.

"You can read too, can't you? Really, this office makes me violently ill. Here are your instructions—comply or not, that's your choice. But we both know you don't have a choice."

Giocondo handed him a single handwritten piece of paper and stood up. He was never asked to reach into his satchel with the proof, his rock. Once viewed, and no matter the passion of the person viewing it, it simply made it impossible to ever believe again. It was like staring at Medusa, except that it was one's belief that was turned to stone, and the body just had to deal with it.

The CEO was visibly shaken, though he wasn't entirely surprised that this data had surfaced. He thought, given the contingency, that he should provide protection to the archeologist twenty-four hours a day. He certainly didn't want anything happening to him before this matter was resolved.

He also didn't seem to shudder in the least when faced with the archeologist's only demands: €5,000,000,000 deposited into an account in India within twelve hours and €50,000,000 every month thereafter, with specific delivery instructions to follow. Giocondo considered these royalty payments, for the cash-wells would continue to gush a weekly tithing. He now considered himself a colossal shareholder in these assets.

"The truth as you call it—it's in a secure location?"

"The only reason I'm here is to shield others from the pain I've suffered. Do you understand that I was looking for further evidence of my belief, not this? I nearly went crazy. I don't want to burden others, and I hope you take care of the poor man beneath you who forced me to share."

"Yes, we're trying to find him now. I think it's best if I provide you security until all of the details are worked out. And where exactly did you make this discovery, Dr. Benvenuto? Were there other witnesses to this great find?"

"I said earlier that no one else knows. And certainly I would expect to be followed, or 'protected,' as you call it."

And with that very brief meeting, Giocondo was escorted out as quickly as he had been ushered into the office. Once on the street, he noticed commotion coming from the nearby train station. Police and ambulance sirens were wailing, and emergency lights flashed in bright blues and reds.

He didn't know that the first employee he shared the truth with had leapt onto the tracks as a train approached only five minutes after seeing the truth. The train did its job by shredding his soul from its worldly body.

The CEO, ignoring Benvenuto's refusal of a personal security team, instructed one of his subordinates to place his two best security personnel, and their accompanying employees, on a team trailing the doctor. This elite team usually managed the CEO's own protection, but given the severity of the information, he was more than happy to reassign them.

Giocondo would be protected, like it or not, for the rest of his life. One of the three employees he shared the truth with would serve as his liaison with the corporation. His demotion to a lowly local unit manager suited all involved.

It was not a dangerous city, but they would not risk anything happening to him until an agreement was firmly in place—nor, for that matter, would they ever risk anything happening to him in the future, even after a formal agreement. Before transferring the €5,000,000,000 into the specified account, the CEO contacted his counterparts, the CEOs of his three largest competitors, all of whom were very troubled by the news.

Neither the CEO nor his equivalents wished to jeopardize everything over what they considered a rather tawdry sum. The CEO was decidedly unimpressed with Benvenuto's assertion that none of his staff back in Sudan had any knowledge of this discovery.

Sudan was a dangerous place. If an entire village was wiped off the face of the earth, it wouldn't exactly raise much attention. And thus the massacre at the site of the momentous unearthing went virtually unnoticed by all.

Chapter 22: Everyone Weep with Me

Seven years and one hundred and sixty days after Giocondo Benvenuto's meeting with the CEO, fate had planned that two weddings of interest were to be celebrated on a late fall Saturday afternoon, one in Praiano and one in Rome. These weddings were to begin at nearly identical times, though no friends or relatives of either party would regret that they couldn't attend them both. Neither groom knew that fate would ultimately introduce them.

In Praiano, it was an overcast, misty day. Not ideal weather for a wedding, but blue-sky weddings in this town were mostly reserved for tourists.

And the weather couldn't have dampened Amalia's mood. All she could think about was her father escorting her down the main aisle to the altar of the St. Gennaro basilica.

In a small mirrored room inside the church, she had gathered with her sister, Francesca, the maid of honor, and her bridesmaids: Juliana, Isabella, and two other friends she had known since early childhood. Joining them in last-minute preparations were Amalia's mother and Ciro's mother, Maria. These two would soon be escorted to their seats of honor at the front of the basilica.

Amalia's lace ivory sheath gown, crafted locally, was expertly fitted to her lean build, closely following the lines of her faultless body. Everyone agreed that Ciro was one lucky man. Her matching lace veil was dainty and just grazed her shoulders. Small white roses encircled the veil and her brow, and her dark hair was tightly pulled back with flowing interwoven braids. Francesca was making the final adjustments to the veil as the ceremony began to draw near.

"You look so beautiful, Amalia. You mustn't start crying

and ruin this perfect look of yours."

"I was thinking about Ciro and how this day might never have happened, and it's so hard not to cry!"

"You must not think of that time," he mother intervened. "Allow yourself to glory in the splendor of this day! By the way, and this might help, I saw Ciro and Ote sneaking out back where they thought they were cleverly hidden, and they were obviously smoking something. I thought they both quit smoking! Ciro's alive and well, dear, and it seems he celebrates!"

They all laughed. Amalia agreed with her mother and staring down at the two-carat emerald-cut diamond set in platinum, remembered a day two months earlier. They were on the Arienzo beach, a beautiful early fall day filled with sun.

They were just lounging at the beach when, during a simple lunch of gnocchi and a locally bottled red wine, Ciro sank to one knee and proposed, stunning her with this too-costly engagement ring. He claimed he had been saving for five years, but she wondered if Gio, in one final noble act, assisted with the purchase.

Drawing attention to oneself with such an impressive diamond wasn't a part of their initial strategy of lying low. Most would reason that someone who loses fifty million Euro might still be looking for it.

As Amalia's mother had reported, Ciro and Ote had indeed escaped outside. They needed to calm their nerves, and so they sought refuge between the church and a mechanical shed, congratulating themselves on what they believed was an undetectable retreat. Here Mary Wanna joined them.

Father Viglianti had seen them as well. He was preparing just above them in the vestibule, donning his ornamental wedding vestments and preparing the sacraments. His window was open, and he was taking great pleasure in the preparations—until he heard Ote and Ciro start talking crazy talk after their joint.

"When you return from the States, Ciro, we need to share our good fortune with our wives. I can't keep this from Juliana much longer. We can't explain away a two hundred thousand Euro boat or that ring or these Rolexes you bought for the groomsmen."

"I think Amalia would look happier than she will on her wedding day! But yes, it's important to have no secrets from our wives. As for the boat, I think it might be a little too much unless we can produce a whale of a tuna to Salvatore. Here, step on that. I don't think we're allowed to have such sinful substances in the basilica!"

Viglianti trembled upon hearing this very upsetting news. He thought they were smarter than this. He wished he could go down there and warn them.

Big diamonds? Rolex watches? Yachts? How could they act so recklessly? When he thought about having to preside over their funeral masses, witnessing the hurt left behind and hearing those mournful cries, he almost couldn't contain himself.

Ciro's wedding dream during his coma, of which he had no memory, was mostly very accurate. The church was overflowing with guests, Amalia's beauty was stunning, and his joy was overwhelming.

Somehow in his dream he hadn't pictured the billionaire Gio accompanying Dr. Neurmer and her daughter, Courtney. Neither Neurmer seemed to have properly recovered from their grief quite yet. Nor had he envisioned Father Viglianti choking up virtually every time he spoke during the sacrament of matrimony.

After the wedding and before the reception, Ciro and Amalia sought out Viglianti. They were both moved by the emotions he had displayed during their wedding. They really did love him more as a friend than as a priest. But he must have slipped off during the commotion of the guests greeting the new couple. In fact, just before the ceremony began he had strangely told Ciro that he wouldn't be able to attend the reception after all, a last-minute thing.

They found him back in the vestibule removing his vestments and securing the vessels while talking quietly on the phone. They startled him as he was ending the call, and he burst into tears.

Father Viglianti had sadly decided that he no choice, and with that call he had given the wheel a spin, except it was unlikely that it would land randomly.

In Rome, the weather was more pleasant, though a bit colder than in Praiano. This basilica was just as opulent as the basilica in Praiano, though its guests were much fewer in number.

The only member of Aprajita's wedding party was her soon to be sister-in-law, Alessio's sister-in-law. They were joined by Alessio's mother, who cradled Ramesh.

Aprajita too looked every bit as stunning as her bridal counterpart in Praiano. She wore an empire gown in the faintest shade of pink, embroidered ever so slightly with yellow flowers. Her hair too was pulled back, but in a simpler style. She wore a pearly braid instead of a veil.

"Did Alessio tell you of the history of your engagement ring?" Alessio's mother asked.

"Yes, yes of course! I don't think I've ever seen him happier than when he told me the story of how your husband gave you this same ring nearly fifty years ago. I will wear this very important ring with the same pride and commitment that you have. I hope you understand how delighted he is to have you back in his life!"

"He is lucky to have you, Aprajita," she said, struggling over the name. "You saw my expression when you arrived at my door with Ramesh. I thought you were a gypsy making house calls using a small child as a prop to sell something. I almost didn't answer but am so glad I did. It was time to quit hating and start loving, and you helped me to realize that. And

I'm so happy that Alessio and Vincenzo have reunited. Thank you for all you have done to restore a family!"

The groom's party consisted of Alessio and his brother, who were still in the process of getting reacquainted. Alessio was firing question after question at Vincenzo, who looked almost exactly like his brother, though he was slightly less fit.

"Tell me about your new position at the Vatican, Vincenzo. I hear only the cardinals, and of course the pope, have a higher position!"

"Work is going fine, no complaints there, but I do work too much, unlike the luckiest realtor in town!"

"I suspected that your tennis game would have diminished, but it seems like you haven't picked up a tennis racquet since we last played!"

"I told you to take it easy on me!"

"I will next time, I promise. I've missed you, dear Vincenzo. Every day I try to think of ways of earning your forgiveness. I love you—please never leave me again!"

The two brothers clutched one another, laughing because they were crying. They would have never dared cry in front of one another growing up, especially once they were in their teens. Now both were fathers and they cried all the time, though this was the first time they had shared tears together.

Soon after, the priest ushered them into the nave before the altar. There was a scattering of guests, perhaps thirty or so, but none from Aprajita's family, though the newlyweds intended to visit them in India very soon. Aprajita was left to walk the aisle on her own without the beautiful organ and choir that was heard about an hour ago in Praiano.

Alessio smiled as widely as Ciro did when he saw his beautiful Aprajita in her gown. He thought to himself that this was just the way a wedding should be. He praised God for answering his prayers. Less than six months ago he was alone, unloved, and empty.

About midway through the exchanging of vows, fate once

again proved cruel. One never knew where the wheel might stop, and as soon as it settled, it began to spin anew.

Just as Aprajita finished her vow to obey, a cell phone rang. *Twinkle, twinkle, little star, how I wonder what you are, up above the world so high, like a diamond in the sky.* The ringtone stirred the guests, given whose cell phone was beckoning.

Aprajita gaped in disbelief at this timing, although she had already been warned that this could happen at any time. Alessio was also in disbelief. He answered because like Father Viglianti, he had no choice. Save for a quick gesture of his hand, he deserted his bride, son, mother, and brother to seek the privacy of the nearby vestibule where he awaited further instruction.

The truth? When his phone twinkled, it was vital that Alessio immediately answer with "*Pronto*" for he had no faith that they would call back.

"*Pronto. Si, si … si … si … Grazie, ciao!*"

And in less than a minute on the phone with the unknown caller, Alessio began his workday. Line two always came first. This time the unknown caller demanded immediate action and seemed especially incensed. Wedding days were no deliverance from this evil. Since he had no choice, it was hi-ho, hi-ho, Alessio.

More books from
Harvard Square Editions:

People and Peppers, Kelvin Christopher James

Gates of Eden, Charles Degelman

Love's Affliction, Fidelis Mkparu

Transoceanic Lights, S. Li

Close, Erika Raskin

Anomie, Jeff Lockwood

Living Treasures, Yang Huang

Nature's Confession, J.L. Morin

A Little Something, Richard Haddaway

Dark Lady of Hollywood, Diane Haithman

Fugue for the Right Hand, Michele Tolela Myers

Growing Up White, James P. Stobaugh

Calling the Dead, R.K. Marfurt

Parallel, Sharon Erby